4.

# All Men Are Lonely Now

*By Francis Clifford*

# *All Men Are*

FRANCIS CLIFFORD

# Lonely Now

Coward-McCann, Inc.
New York

41,802

*He is not he; she is not she;*
*they are not they.*

# Part One ]

All men are lonely now.
This is the hour when no man has a friend.

—EDNA ST. VINCENT MILLAY

*  *  *  *  *

I do not like being moved: for the will is
    excited; and action
Is a most dangerous thing; I tremble for
    something factitious,
Some malpractice of heart and illegitimate
    process;
We're so prone to these things with our
    terrible notions of duty.

—ARTHUR HUGH CLOUGH

# Chapter 1 ]

**A**T first they saw the lightning. And then they heard the thunder. And then, as the rain swept over the lake, they entered the cottage and made love.

Afterward, spent, their limbs slack, she said: "Give me a cigarette, will you?" Her voice was low, as if that sudden cry of ecstasy minutes before had constricted her throat. The rain was drumming on the roof and Lancaster didn't move. She waited a few moments, then turned her head, at the same time squeezing him gently on the thigh. "David," she said.

"Yes?"

"Remember me?"

He looked at her with mock gravity, affecting a frown. "The face is familiar."

"I hate you."

"So soon?"

"I asked for a cigarette."

"Sorry."

He reached for the bedside table, fumbled two filtertips from an open pack and lit them both. Tiny beads of perspiration were clustered along the line of the girl's upper lip and he brushed them away with his mouth before giving her one of the cigarettes.

"It's Catherine, isn't it? Catherine Tierney?"

"Oh I hate you," she repeated evenly.

"Then I want to be hated."

"Don't joke. Not any more."

"You'll never grow up if you believe in love."

He nestled his head against hers, her black hair crushed by the side of his face, and blew smoke toward the ceiling. Lightning flickered behind the curtained windows but the thunder took a long time to sound; and when it came it was fainter, the storm drifting eastward. Only the rain persisted, heavy and sullen, isolating them from the rest of Ireland, from far-off London, Weapons Coordination, the rest of the world.

Twice before she had been here—a month ago, first, and again the previous weekend. The cottage was small, white, single-storied, with a thatched roof and a blue front door: there was one bedroom, a bathroom, and a kitchen in which they sometimes ate. A cinder path curved from the road to the blue door between unkempt rosebushes, and the broken stone walls which led down to the lakeside reeds at the back enclosed nothing more than grass. "I got it for a song," Lancaster had told her. "Add the cost of putting the bathroom in and slapping on some paint and collecting a few sticks of furniture, and it still came to less than four figures. Incredible, but true."

He had mentioned this one summer evening in his Chelsea flat, before they had slept together. Not that his having a place somewhere in Connemara was in any way a secret at

Weapons Coordination. "My bolt hole," he called it. "Five hours from London and you put the clock back a hundred years. And the trout in Lochmor are all aspiring record-breakers." But he hadn't fished when she had been with him. His rods were propped inside the front door and she had teased him about them. "Do they fool all the girls?" she had asked the previous weekend. And he'd answered lightly: "Every time," adding, "No one's ever been here except you."

Now they lay naked together, listening to the rain, finishing their cigarettes. Catherine was slim, small-boned, her skin so pale that Lancaster's seemed almost swarthy by comparison. He was on the tall side, broad-shouldered, muscular, with a smudge of brown hair between his nipples that was lighter than the close-cropped mat that ended in a widow's peak on his forehead. They remained for several minutes without speaking and sometimes he gazed along the length of her body, marveling, fondling her gently. It was difficult to believe that, in twenty-four hours' time, she'd be calling him "Mr. Lancaster" again, saying perhaps, "Yes, he's free," if he wanted to see Conway, or coming formally into his own office on those high heels of hers with some file or other.

They knew about the cottage at Weapons Coordination, but not about this. Nobody did. This was private.

"You're gorgeous," he said, and she smiled at him, raising a hand to touch his face.

"What's the time?"

"About noon." He looked at his watch. "Twelve-fourteen, to be precise. We'll go over to the hotel just as soon as you say. It sounds as if the rain's easing."

He swung himself off the bed and pulled the curtains

[ 13 ]

aside. Thunder growled a vague diapason in the distance but the clouds had dragged clear of the hills beyond the lake.

"Blue sky coming up. It'll be fine soon."

He was the first to dress. When he had finished he sat on the end of the bed and watched her comb her hair before the mirror. Like most of the furniture, he had picked up the mirror in the local auction rooms for next to nothing. Connemara was slowly dying, house by house, village by village: only the beauty and the sadness were permanent. In another twenty years, people said, there would be little else left except the hotels and the weekend shooting and fishing lodges and the big houses rescued from decay by wealthy foreigners.

"There's irony for you," Lancaster had remarked during that first, heady weekend.

"Why irony?"

"Because for something like eight hundred years the Irish fought to get the British out. And now, within a lifetime of independence, they're having to get out themselves. What's more, the British are coming back—the British and the Americans and the Germans. Your ancestors would turn in their graves with despair."

"I've no Irish blood."

"With a name like Tierney?"

"Not that I'm aware. Not a drop."

"Then I've put the wrong label on you."

"I'm not sure that I care to be labeled."

"Weapons Coordination might consider that a sign of potential weakness. They want us labeled *and* dedicated."

"I know what Weapons Coordination want. Don't remind me."

"They're ten million miles away."

"Let's keep it like that. Monday will come soon enough."

She had joined the department about six months earlier, in March. George Conway's secretary had transferred to the Minister's personal staff and the establishment people sent him Catherine as a replacement. The first time she entered Lancaster's office he was on the telephone, engrossed, and he barely noticed her. Yet within a week he was studying her retreating back as she left his desk and made for the door, admiring her long slender legs, fascinated by her slightly swaying walk, disturbed in the familiar way. She was soft-spoken, unflustered, with eyes and mouth quick to smile, the eyes very blue and large, the mouth generous and scarcely painted. Twenty-seven, he had reckoned; there or thereabouts.

Before Easter she had dined with him and soon they were meeting regularly. But his early approaches foundered with the kisses. There was always a moment when he was firmly restrained; and there were others when she seemed curiously withdrawn, solemn, as if she were brooding. He couldn't fathom her in those initial weeks, though that was part of the fascination, part of the challenge. They never left the office together, parting with a casual "Good night" on the outer steps if chance happened to bring them down in the lift at the same time, dining in small restaurants clear off the beaten track. It was her suggestion that they do so and he agreed, partly because he saw promise in it, partly because he preferred to be spared the inevitability of Conway's disapproval. She made no bones about her reasons, which stemmed from Conway too. "He hates your guts—you know that. And he's difficult enough to work for as it is. He'd make things pretty intolerable for me if he so much as guessed."

Conway virtually ran the department these days; more and more McBride seemed to be letting him have the reins. A day was soon coming when the Old Man would ease himself out altogether, collect his knighthood and go. And Lancaster didn't relish the prospect. Personal antagonism apart, Conway would make everything even more demanding than it already was.

He hadn't lied to Catherine; no other woman had come with him to Connemara. When he joined Weapons Coordination McBride had said: "This place is like the confessional, David. Remember that, at all times and in all places." But he hadn't needed telling. Caution had become a habit; three years with the Inter-Services Security group had conditioned him. Catherine was the first with whom he felt safe enough to be spared the consequences of some unguarded utterance or momentary indiscretion. He had never been able to abandon himself so utterly as with her. Like him she was one of a trusted few, vetted and cleared by a complex pattern of security procedures before she ever set foot in the slightly dingy fifth-floor offices where the department was housed. When she eventually yielded to him in his Bramerton Street flat he achieved more than an easing of his physical needs: he knew that with her he could at last experience a degree of release from the discipline that had long gripped his mind like a vise.

"Ready?" he asked now, and she nodded, pausing only

to drop a comb, compact and lipstick into his breast pocket. It was often her way: here she never carried a bag.

They went out to the car, picking their way around the rain pools in the cinders. Bruised-looking streamers of cloud obscured the sun, and the eastern horizon was dark and mottled; but the blue was slowly filling in. They were half-way to the Lake Hotel before either of them spoke. Then, glancing sidelong, Lancaster said: "A penny for them."

"Huh?"

"You were dreaming again."

"Was I?" She could still lose herself where he couldn't follow; still lock him out. "It was nothing."

"You're a Gael, all right. A brooding, melancholy, layers-deep Gael."

"Nonsense."

"Beautiful, too."

At last she smiled back. He drove fast through the rain-bow weather in the red, rented Volvo saloon. Nothing stood between the cottage and the hotel except a succession of low walls and a few clumps of trees spaced haphazardly over the two miles. The lake was absolutely still, like glass, the water on the far side heavy with the weight of the re-flected hills. Some stray sheep once made Lancaster brake, but otherwise the road was deserted: in this part of the world you could often motor for half an hour without seeing another car. The only vehicle parked in the hotel's forecourt when they swung in was a mud-spattered Land Rover.

"Fletcher's here," Catherine said.

"Never absent, never late—that's Fletcher." Fletcher farmed nearby.

The Lake Hotel was a converted mansion—gray-walled, slate-roofed, its slightly down-at-heel façade so smothered with ivy that the windows looked dark and sunken. Given the chance, nature would win here yet. But the interior was cheerful, snug, the smell of damp kept at bay by glowing turf fires. Sure enough, Fletcher was installed, alone, perched on the self-same stool in the bar from which he'd waved a boozy farewell last night.

"Hallo," Lancaster said. "I reckon you'll take root in that spot one of these days."

"You wouldn't dare imply a slander like that if you were on your own. I'd have your hide off." Fletcher was huge: big trunk, thick legs, meaty shoulders straining the seams of his tweed jacket. Pouchy middle-aged eyes took their deliberate fill of Catherine. "Don't you think I would?"

"I'm sure you're not a violent man, Mr. Fletcher."

"Oh?" It seemed to gratify him. "You're a real disarmer. . . . What's your poison?"

"I'd like a gin, please."

"Gin and tonic?"

"Please."

Fletcher shifted heavily on the stool. "And you, David? I'm not often as magnanimous, so take advantage of it."

"I'll have a beer, thanks."

"A *what?*"

"A beer."

"Beer," Fletcher snorted, "is for washing down cars and fattening pigs. You can do better than that, surely?"

"A beer will suit me fine."

"God in heaven." Fletcher ran both hands over his bald,

brick-colored scalp and called: "Pat. . . . How about a little service, Pat?"

The barman had one of those narrow faces that seemed incapable of any great range of expression. He had nicked himself shaving and there was blood on his collar. "Morning, Mr. Lancaster . . . morning, miss."

Lancaster said, "Looks as if you're in for a quiet day."

"They'll be along now the storm's blown over. The weather never beat a Galway man yet."

"Bloody parochialism," Fletcher growled. "That's the curse of this country. If it isn't a Galway man it's a Kerry man, and if it isn't a Kerry man it's a Cork man, or a lad from Donegal or Sligo or wherever."

As always the slightly overloud voice came from well back in the throat, but Lancaster had never seen Fletcher drunk. He seemed to remain permanently on the brink, no matter what the hour, no matter how much whiskey he'd taken. But he wasn't a person with whom one could be at ease.

"Look at me," he was booming on. "I'm British first, English second, Cornish third. So what? I don't go beating my breast about it. 'The weather never beat a Galway man yet' —cock. Ask my foreman Sean how many Galway invincibles missed work at my place last time the skies opened like to-day." He drank almost angrily. "Don't give me the romantic soft soap, Pat, there's a good lad."

They suffered his monopoly for ten long minutes. He was a boor, with all the arrogance of the half-educated. Then, mercifully, people began to arrive, coming from the outlying houses and Kilvarna village, regulars, familiar faces, men in raincoats and gumboots, men in their Sunday outfits, trou-

[ 19 ]

sers creased at the knees after Mass, men who'd walked or
cycled or traveled by car. Invariably men, an hour or so
later than usual, determined to make up lost time.

"When are you off to London, David?" Fletcher demanded.

"This evening."

"And when do we see you again?"

"That depends."

"Next weekend? If you feel like a shoot the guns will be
ready."

"Thanks."

"Bring some more books over, whenever it is."

"I'll try."

"Do more than try; make a point of it. Otherwise I'll never
forgive you." The bloodshot stare, the coarse, veined face.
"Simple pleasures, young lady, simple pleasures, that's all.
The best kind of book is officially not for Irish eyes, so I have
to resort to using my friends."

They parted from him and went into the dining room. No
one else was there. It was as if a pressure had been lifted
from the senses. They sat at a window table and Oonagh, the
barman's sister, served them. There were sporting prints on
the walls and, above the fireplace, an enormous Lochmor
trout in a glass case: nineteen and a quarter pounds, the
legend stated.

"What did you last bring Fletcher?"

"*August Is a Wicked Month* and *Fanny Hill.*"

Catherine laughed. "His bark must be worse than his bite."

"All the same," Lancaster shrugged, "he somehow suc-
ceeds in making me feel like a pimp."

"Why do it, then?"

"I don't think I will any more."

They were closest, their relationship most nearly itself, when there and then were all that mattered; but time was running out. Soon they would have to go, pack, start for the airport.

"I love you," Catherine said.

"Careful," Lancaster wagged a finger.

"You know it."

They drank their coffee in the lounge. The fire there had burned low; only a glimmer showed through the crusted white ash. Lancaster bent to stoke it. Logs were stacked on one side of the hearth, turf bars on the other. As he picked up a couple of logs, Catherine said urgently: "Use the turf, David." But she was too late; he had dropped the wood in. Dust flew and the bark crackled. Lancaster squatted in front of the grate, watching the flames begin to lick. A minute must have elapsed before he straightened up and joined her.

"You get a bit of life with wood."

"Someone once told me you can hear the insects scream."

"Rubbish."

"You can see them run, though."

"Maybe."

"What ran just then?"

"I wasn't watching."

"Liar," she said gently.

"If you say so."

As he sipped his coffee she glimpsed once again those muscles in the jaws. He was always progressively more tense as the weekend ebbed, but she hadn't noticed the signs so early before. They left the hotel without going through the bar and he drove her back to the cottage. He was unusually quiet, even when he made love to her for the third time that day; quiet yet violent. Afterward they packed and he locked up. Then she climbed into the Volvo beside him and they started on the long journey across the country's heart to Dublin.

A few boats were out on the lake. The water was quickly behind them; Kilvarna as well, huddled close to itself as if for protection. The roads and lanes were as empty as ever. Lancaster headed for Ballinasloe, taking the familiar route, sadness woven into the desolate splendor of the land in the warm, clear light. Green and brown and gray; grass and bog and rock. Near Monivea the storm had stripped the blossoms from the wild fuchsia in the hedgerows and it looked as if blood filled the ditches.

Catherine switched the radio on and Sinatra came through.

> "When I was thirty-five
> It was a *very* good year . . ."

"Was it, David?"

"Too long ago to remember."

"Nonsense."

"Long, long ago," he insisted.

"You forget I've seen your file. You're thirty-eight."

"No comment."

"Did their hair come undone?"

"That was at twenty-one. You've muddled the lyric."

"I'm not talking about the lyric."

"There's never been a year like this," Lancaster said. She would have him in love with her yet—and for once the possibility didn't scare him. But love was a language he had never learned.

Time passed. Ballinasloe came and went, then Tullamore, then Edenderry, with lonely places in between that seemed to have forgotten the world and to have been forgotten by it. Peace and safety, the old passions spent, reality no more matching the nightmares of the mind—that was Ireland now. Lancaster drove on. The countryside had lost its harshness. Here it was lush and the light was shrinking fast. They had picked up other traffic and he let it set the pace. There was time enough, time to spare. Presently Maynooth hemmed them in, Maynooth where priests were made: others could be dedicated, too.

"Hungry?"

"So-so."

"Journey's end almost in sight."

Three hours after leaving Kilvarna there were signs directing them to the airport. Lancaster left the car in the lee of the main building, settled with the hire firm's duty clerk, saw the baggage weighed, then took Catherine up to the restaurant. Heads turned as she entered; she had that quality. Often when he observed the interest of strangers in her he did so with a proprietary glow of pleasure, but tomorrow was pressing and a part of him was restless, tension returning with the insistence of an ineradicable fever. The crowded restaurant, the clash of voices, the family at the neighboring table with their middle-class London accents, the occasional turboprop whine in the darkness outside—escape was never more than partial, never more than temporary.

"One of their people has defected," McBride had told him late on Friday afternoon. "An East German, I gather, name of Adler. And if first reports are correct they know something about Roman Candle. . . . No, no, stick to your personal arrangements. I don't believe in panic stations. If any damage has been done a weekend drama won't set it right. And we'll have the facts by Monday."

For forty-eight hours Lancaster had carried McBride's bombshell with him, totally free of it only during the crises when nothing existed for him except Catherine's body locked in frenzy with his own. Now, increasingly, the implications filled his mind. Only with difficulty could he match her small talk or produce a smile. And she noticed.

"Who said I was the broody one?"

They finished eating and waited for their flight to be called. By the time they had walked across the floodlit apron to the aircraft and belted themselves in he was almost completely silent. They were airborne before she tackled him.

"What's the matter, David?"

"Matter?"

"Is it me?"

"God, no." He shook his head. "What a fool thing to ask."

"You've gone as quiet as the grave."

"Thinking, that's all."

"What about?"

"The Old Man wants to see me in the morning."

"Is that so terrible?"

"You never know, do you?" he countered, then shrugged, raising the ghost of a grin. "Sorry."

He pressed her hand. All the signs were that a witch hunt

was about to begin. A rumor as serious as this was enough to start Conway jumping; even a rumor.

"Sorry," he repeated. "Let's see if I can get you something to drink. . . . Gin, is it?"

On the other side of the gangway a woman nursed a fretful child; it cried now and again as if for no other reason than that it was frightened already of the pain and the passion that would consume it before the endless dark. And through the windows the ice-blue stars were vast, like diamonds.

# Chapter 2 ] 🦋

RUTH Smart, McBride's plump secretary, was saying briskly: "Would you come along now, Mr. Lancaster?"

"Right away?" It was barely nine-thirty.

"Please."

"Very well."

Lancaster crossed the room and put his head around the door of his own secretary's built-in wood and glass cubicle. "I'll be with the Old Man, Margaret."

Her typewriter had apparently jammed and she was fiddling angrily with the carriage. Normally he might have tried to help, or perhaps said something like, "Cheer up. You'll find the week gets better as it goes along." But today she could stew in her own Monday-morning juice.

"The Old Man," he repeated.

She shot him an exasperated glance. "We all have our problems," she retorted with unaccustomed venom. She thumped the machine on the desk and Lancaster went out into the corridor. McBride's office was at the far end. Ruth gave him her Mona Lisa smile as he entered, the one she always seemed to reserve exclusively for him, and merely said: "You can go on through."

He didn't knock. McBride was standing by the corner window, rolled umbrella in a two-handed grip, humming quietly to himself. Lancaster paused, holding the door ajar. A couple of pigeons waddled on the worn sill. McBride tapped the glass with the tip of the umbrella and the pigeons lifted off, flapping away above the traffic that wheeled endlessly out of Trafalgar Square and the Strand into Whitehall. McBride gave them a second or two's grace, then raised the umbrella into a firing position, squinted along its length and twice jerked fractionally as if his right shoulder had absorbed a double kick.

"Good morning, sir," Lancaster said.

"Ah, good morning, David." He seemed quite unperturbed, and Lancaster suddenly had the feeling that McBride had known he'd been there all along. "I fancy I'd have missed—I really do." The gentle Scottish voice sounded almost pained. He hooked the umbrella on the rack behind his swivel chair. "Old men ought to know when to quit—eh, David?"

He looked tired, but then he always did. And grave, though that was normal too. He had known so much, knew so much, was bound by so many granite decisions. But his eyes occasionally redeemed the natural solemnity of his features: when he smiled it was with his eyes, whereas Conway used only his lips. And, outwardly, nothing ever rattled him. Tired he might be; grave, yes. But calm, always calm, always considerate. Stephen Hearne had once quipped that the Old Man's calm was like the peace of God because it passed all understanding, and the joke was intended as a compliment.

McBride sat down, gesturing to Lancaster to follow suit.

"George Conway's joining us, so if you don't mind we'll wait for him. This fellow Adler is still closeted with the Americans in Berlin and they haven't put him on show yet, not even for their friends. George was over there yesterday and the day before, and we've both been on the scrambler half the night. We're not much farther forward, but it doesn't look too good, David." He leaned back, tapping his fingertips together, and hummed a few tuneless bars. And then, incredibly, he asked: "What sort of weekend did you have?"

"Fair."

"Across the water?"

"Yes."

"How was the fishing?"

"It wasn't." Lancaster lit a cigarette. McBride would never cease to amaze him. "About Roman Candle," he began anxiously. "Is it a case of their having got wind of the broad theory of the thing, or is the situation worse than that?"

"Worse, it seems."

"Performance data?"

"Very possibly."

"Christ."

A buzzer sounded and McBride picked up the black telephone. "Who? . . . No, no, not now. Tell him I'll call back. Meanwhile remind Mr. Conway that we're expecting him, will you? . . . Oh, is he?"

The door opened as he was hanging up and Conway came in. Conway was everything McBride was not—stocky, neatly dressed, carefully groomed. He was about ten years Lancaster's senior. McBride got a muttered "Sorry," but Lancaster he ignored.

He pulled a chair up to the desk and placed a plain green folder in front of him. Except for slightly raw-rimmed eyes, his appearance was much the same as usual. In manner he reminded Lancaster of one of his masters at school—patronizing, demanding, watchful.

McBride said immediately: "I've had another word with the Minister."

"Will he play?"

"He's promised to do everything he can."

"He'd better. Adler's being flown to the States tonight. He'll be even more inaccessible once he's there. All I want is an hour with him first."

McBride nodded. A faint rumble of traffic reached the high-ceilinged room.

"David's pretty much in the dark, by the way. He'd find it helpful if you explained what's been happening."

"It's simple enough." Conway turned grudgingly. It might have been his office already, his meeting. "The Americans are busy pumping Adler dry on their own account. We've been pressing for facilities to do the same—unsuccessfully, so far."

"Who precisely is he?"

"Adler? Until last Wednesday he was a full colonel on the active list of the G.R.U."

Lancaster frowned. "I thought he was German. It's a German name. What's a German doing in Russian Military Intelligence?"

"His mother was Russian. He was educated in Russia, served in the Red Army, married a Russian. For the last eighteen months he's been stationed in Potsdam."

"Is that where he crossed? In Berlin?"

"To the best of my knowledge." Conway's tone implied: Who cares about *that*?

McBride said quietly: "All our evidence is secondhand, David. None of our people has had an opportunity to get near him. But we do know that in the course of the preliminary investigations Adler has referred to Roman Candle. We *were* told that much." He pursed his lips ruefully. "George has ferreted out his personal background, and one or two other details have come our way privately."

"Such as?"

"Such as," Conway answered, "the fact that Woomera range trials were also mentioned."

"In relation to Roman Candle?"

"Apparently."

Lancaster knocked ash into McBride's big glass tray. "Who did you get this from?"

"Broom—C.I.A. But only out of the side of his mouth. Find 'ems, keep 'ems—that's the American line with Adler at the moment. And if the past is any guide they won't be all that scrupulous about where their questions stop. They'll pick his brains on Candle by way of a bonus."

"That can't be helped." This was McBride, with a lift of his stooped shoulders.

"It's bloody monstrous."

"The monstrous grows more normal every day, George. And we aren't exactly blameless in that respect, as you very well know. But we do have a right, an urgent right, to put ourselves equally in the picture about one of our own weapons."

[ 30 ]

"Unless the Minister starts cracking a whip we'll be kept waiting until Hell turns Methodist."

"He's seeing the P.M. He can hardly do more."

Conway shifted position irritably. "If the Americans can be persuaded to route Adler's plane via London we can tackle him here, at the airport. All the interested parties can." He glanced coldly at Lancaster. The Old Man never showed his feelings; feelings were too vulgar. But Conway couldn't mask them for long, particularly when a crisis was looming. "Have you anything brilliant to say?"

Lancaster rode the sarcasm as best he could. "There's been no mention of Discus?"

"Not to me."

"That doesn't necessarily put it in the clear."

"God help us if it isn't. This alone is damaging—"

"What exactly did Broom spill?"

"Basically that Adler had referred to a ground-to-air missile for use against low-flying aircraft."

"But that's as inconclusive as could be," Lancaster protested. "Pretty well every national defense effort this side of the Curtain—"

"Laser beam?" Conway snapped. "Proximity fuse? Cluster scatter? If that isn't Candle, tell me what is."

Lancaster crushed the remains of his cigarette in the tray. Always in Weapons Coordination there existed a hovering sense of doom, a feeling that sometime, somehow, the sky could fall. One lived with it, just as for long periods people could carry a fatal germ quiescent in their bodies without harm to themselves. Throughout the weekend he had fought against believing in a man called Adler and the repercussions that might spread beyond this room, this office, as a result of him; spread and rebound again like ripples off a bank. But now the effort was dead.

"Broom told you all this?"

"In as many words, yes. And C.I.A. aren't slouches in Europe. They're good here. Second to none."

McBride cleared his throat. "How far Adler can enlighten us remains to be seen. But one thing is already beyond dispute—there's been a leak. Possibly a massive leak."

"And fast, too." Conway flipped open the green folder, eyes intent as he checked his facts. He was like an artist in that his talent was constantly to disturb. "The first test-firing at Woomera was in late July, on the twenty-fourth. It's now . . . what?—nine weeks since testing began, and already there's a certain gentleman from across the way with knowledge of it. That's fast by any standard." He rose abruptly and stared out of the window. "God," he said, and went on staring, for all the world as if he'd just grasped the full significance of what they'd been discussing. Then, with a change of voice: "What kind of bastard does these things?"

A horn blared below, reaching them like a throttled cry. And McBride brooded aloud: "Someone will always bend if the wind is right."

"Not here," Lancaster said. "I can't swallow that." He shook his head.

"Why not?" Conway demanded.

"We're too close-knit. Too compact. And besides—"

"We're as open to being tapped as any other department. And more worth the tapping."

Lancaster let a shrug answer for him, conveying what

words could not: that to his mind Weapons Coordination was an elite.

"We're wide open," Conway insisted. "To pretend otherwise is to stick one's head in the bloody ground."

"But so is Research and Development wide open, so is Guildford, so is the Minister's own Liaison Section and so is Woomera."

"Not to the same extent. For instance, the Woomera group doesn't have the collated material. And Guildford isn't on the Round Robin list."

"I'm well aware of the drill."

"And I'm well aware that if there's a burglar in the neighborhood I don't exclude the need to look under my own bed."

Lancaster said heatedly: "You don't know what Adler's in possession of yet."

"There's been a leak," Conway glared. "That's enough for me. If Roman Candle is even partially up the spout it's vital to prevent Discus from going the same way."

McBride's tone was only minutely reproving. "It doesn't *have* to be us, George. It doesn't automatically follow, you know."

His buzzer sounded again. "Yes?" he asked wearily into the phone. "All right, put him through." There was a click and he said: "Good morning. . . . Yes, yes, that's quite correct." After which he listened for what seemed a considerable time, once saying, "No, I hadn't been informed," and later, "Interesting, most interesting. . . . Thank you." Then he rang off and gazed across the desk as if he couldn't remember the point he'd been making.

But he did, and he said: "I can't speak for other departments. But I fully understand how David feels about Weapons Coordination. There's always been such a good spirit here . . . *such* a good spirit." For a moment he seemed quite the wrong man to be sitting in that swivel chair; inadequate, tired, old. "And one gets accustomed to loyalty. One begins to take it for granted—and that, of course, is contrary to the cardinal rule. Which, in turn, is part of the tragedy."

Conway was on edge; he couldn't stand this kind of thing. "I realize it goes against the grain, but the fact remains that someone has sold out. Even if it were only to the extent of a couple of linkage screws, immediate ministerial security action is essential."

To Conway's evident surprise McBride said: "Special Branch has already been given instructions. I was coming to that, George." He gestured apologetically before glancing in Lancaster's direction. "This is going to be distasteful, David, but they've asked for a working contact with us and I've decided that you're best qualified to act in that capacity."

Lancaster nodded, taken aback.

"Someone called Sloan will be getting in touch with you. A Detective Superintendent Sloan."

"Isn't this a bit unorthodox?"

"Not in the circumstances."

"Very well."

"How long the Americans intend keeping Adler under their hat is impossible to say. With luck we'll soon be able to tackle him ourselves. But he doesn't exist outside these four walls of mine—is that understood? At least, not for the present he doesn't. And nobody in the department is to have an inkling they're under the microscope." McBride smiled thinly, as if to hide some bitter hurt. "Have I made myself clear?"

"Yes."

"Cooperate with Sloan. Take your instructions from him. It's been agreed that he'll approach you privately. There will be a temporary circulation curtailment of the yellows, but otherwise the office continues to function as if nothing had happened. And remember, as far as Sloan is concerned, we're all equally in the same boat. That's sure to be his line."

Lancaster hesitated, then got up. If he asked one question he might finish by asking a hundred. And McBride had as good as intimated the meeting was at an end. A nod, a kind of sudden loss of interest—that was his way of doing it.

"I'll be speaking to you again shortly, David."

"Right."

For some reason it seemed a long way to the heavy mahogany door. Ruth said: "Will Mr. Conway be out soon, d'you know?" and he spread his hands by way of answer. Alone in the corridor he stood motionless for a short while, deep in thought, then started toward his own office. He was halfway there when Catherine emerged from Conway's room, colliding with him, gripping him on the arm to steady herself. She was laughing as their eyes met.

"*Mr.* Lancaster—this is so sudden."

Stephen Hearne was just behind her; Lancaster barely noticed in time. "Sorry," he exclaimed as casually as he could. "Are you hurt?"

"Not at all."

"Fair's fair," Hearne protested brightly. "I thought this dance was mine."

"Sure?" Lancaster asked Catherine.

"Quite sure. It was my fault, anyway." Then, for devilment's sake: "Did you have a nice weekend?"

"Fine," he nodded. "Just fine." And left them, a shade too quickly perhaps.

Margaret wasn't in her cubicle when he returned. He walked around behind his desk and looked down into Whitehall, filled with an enormous envy for the imagined simplicity of other people's lives. Now the probing would begin, the clinical checking back, the reassessment of friends, habits, interests, bank accounts—all that. The business of really trusting no one and not being trusted was about to be given fresh emphasis. And overriding everything was the growing certainty that Roman Candle's value was already diminished: Conway had gleaned enough to put that beyond dispute.

"Your coffee, Mr. Lancaster."

His skin prickled; he hadn't heard Margaret arrive. "Thanks," he grunted, but remained where he was, watching the busy pavements below. Adler would have come willingly out of his hole, eager to please, eager to unload. He was a gift, Adler, the kind who triggered chain reactions and shook the whole delicate balance. But gifts were rare: Special Branch could expect nothing to match him. They'd be starting from scratch, groping, feeling their way. Guildford, Research and Development, the Liaison Section, Woomera, Weapons Coordination . . . it could be anybody, anywhere.

He faced the room and sat down, sipped the sweetened

coffee. Anybody. His broad-bottomed secretary, for instance. McBride had never said a truer word; for the time being they were all in the same boat. No one was what he or she appeared to be—not incontrovertibly, not even Margaret, still dickering with her typewriter as if she alone were burdened with troubles. . . .

With an effort he checked the way his mind was working. The feel of Catherine's grip still lingered on his arm and all at once he had a yearning to be spared involvement in whatever was coming, an intense desire for nothing more than her company, her body. But now it was Kilvarna and the peace of the cottage that were all those million miles away.

# Chapter 3 ] ✨

**T**HE telephone rang that evening within minutes of Lancaster's reaching his flat in Bramerton Street, promptly enough for him to wonder if someone had reported his arrival. Nothing was normal any more and already it was beginning to show, if only in that his imagination was alerted.

"Yes?"

"Mr. Lancaster?"

"That's correct."

"My name's Sloan." The voice was hoarse. "I wondered when it would be convenient for me to call."

"Now, if you wish."

"In about a quarter of an hour?"

"Suits me. I'm on the second floor. Press the downstairs bell and walk up."

"Thank you, Mr. Lancaster. I'll do that."

"You know the address, of course?"

"Oh yes."

Sloan was coughing as he rang off. Lancaster poured himself a Scotch and settled in a chair to wait, giving the *Evening Standard* a chance to distract him. But he couldn't get beyond the headlines; too much intruded, keeing him torn between Conway's secondhand disclosures and the Old Man's having elected that he should act as a go-between. He'd liaised with Special Branch once before, during his time with the Inter-Services Security group, and it hadn't been a comfortable experience. That was when the Walker affair had come to its ugly head. Gilligan had been his contact then, Detective Superintendent Gilligan, a mercurial individual with an icy capacity for ruthlessness: he laughed with his shoulders, Lancaster remembered. "Odd, isn't it?" he'd remarked afterward. "When the English are outraged they fly into a terrible calm."

All except Conway, Lancaster thought. Day long, Conway had been unbearable. But he'd achieved the essential —or, rather, the P.M. had finally achieved it for him. Adler's estimated arrival time at London Airport was seventhirty. Conway would be at the airport now, he and certain others, waiting, almost strangers even to themselves. And soon he'd know better to what extent Roman Candle was compromised and whether so much as a whisper of the existence of Discus had followed it. Which was one side of the coin: the other was Sloan's. "Keep me posted, David," the Old Man's parting words had been in midafternoon, and behind the drawn smile was a hint of command, a kind of weary determination to demonstrate that the department was still his responsibility.

A car pulled up in the quiet street. Lancaster rose and glanced down, but it was the woman next door arriving with her yapping Pekingese. On reflection he guessed that Sloan would probably come on foot, and he guessed right. At ten past seven, just as he was toying with the idea of another whiskey, his bell rang. Without haste he went onto the landing and looked over at the man turning at the foot of the second flight. Raincoat, soft hat, briefcase—Sloan could have been calling to flog an encyclopedia.

"Good evening," he said, catching sight of Lancaster while still on the stairs.

"Good evening. Come along up."

He was about the same height as Lancaster, but slimmer, and his face was long and narrow, the eyes particularly close together. At first sight he didn't look the brightest of people. He started coughing as they shook hands and Lancaster sympathized: "That doesn't sound too healthy."

"It's a brute, and no mistake."

"I've the very thing for it. Scotch."

"I won't say no." False teeth as he smiled, with pale, tell-tale gums; sparse, mousy hair now that his hat was off. He shed his raincoat and carried the briefcase through into the living room. "I suppose we'd better get the formalities over, Mr. Lancaster. Sloan, Superintendent Charles Sloan," and he produced a plastic-enclosed card by way of proof.

Lancaster nodded dutifully. "Grab a chair while I fix you a whiskey. How are you taking it—medicinally or for pleasure?"

"With water, please."

"Ice?"

"No, thanks."

Lancaster poured a large measure, more generous than the one for himself. "Well, here's luck."

"Cheers."

Sloan looked about him as he swallowed. He had continued to stand. Beside the clock on the mantelshelf was a note which read: *Where have you been all this time, David?*

*What have you been up to? Ring and tell me. The number's
still the same—Linda.* And Sloan's swift survey of the room
delayed fractionally before continuing. The squeezed-
together eyes were quick and on the go. Furniture, record
player, bric-a-brac, crowded bookcases, Gauguin and Ma-
tisse prints—he was taking it all in.

"A nice place," he said with what could have been envy.
"Very nice."

"It's convenient, which is the main thing."

"Have you been here long?"

"Five years. . . . Whereabouts are you?"

"Hampstead—when I get a chance, that is." He coughed
again, stooping as the spasm shook him.

"Let's get the weight off our feet, shall we?" Lancaster
suggested.

They sat in the deep chairs on either side of a long coffee-
table and Lancaster switched on another bar of the electric
fire. A lengthy pause ensued, a kind of mutual uncertainty,
and Lancaster wondered whether to continue with the brit-
tle preliminaries or to broach the purpose of Sloan's visit.
But Sloan made the choice.

"How well have you been briefed about what I'm after?"

"I was told you'd contact me—no more than that."

"I see." Sloan frowned. The fire pinged as the glow yel-
lowed. "Then it looks as if we'll both be asking questions."

"Very likely. I've certainly got a few of my own." With
Gilligan there had always been an underlying hint of menace, but there was none with Sloan. Yet anybody from Special Branch was best not rubbed the wrong way, and Lancaster added as a palliative: "Go ahead, though. I'm all
yours."

"Am I right in believing that such information as you have has come about as a result of a blow-back from the other side?"

"Quite right."

"And that the full extent of the blow-back isn't yet known?"

"Not yet. But the source is being tackled at London Airport this evening."

"Meaning Adler?" Sloan said, disposing of unnecessary mystery.

"Yes."

"By your Mr. Conway?"

"On behalf of Weapons Coordination, yes."

"As I understand it the first indications are that one specific weapon has been referred to."

"That's correct."

"Roman Candle?"

Lancaster nodded. Sloan had clearly done some basic homework.

"Discus—correct me if I'm wrong—is a more advanced version of Roman Candle?"

"Not really. They have a number of features in common, but in other respects Discus is quite revolutionary. It's early days yet, but Discus *could* be the ultimate in ground-to-air missiles. At present, though, it's more theory than fact. Meanwhile Roman Candle is certainly the most sophisticated weapon of its kind yet proved."

"They're both from the Guildford stable? That's what I'm getting at."

"Guildford in association with Research and Development."

"Is that the only development overlap?"

"No, there are commercial overlaps as well. But those are of a strictly limited nature." Lancaster spread his hands. "I'm not really qualified to answer with any accuracy. This isn't my line. Some private contracting is more or less inevitable, even during the development stage, but it's always undertaken completely out of context."

Sloan sipped his whiskey, squinting down his white, pinched nose. "I should explain, Mr. Lancaster, that my own inquiries will be confined to Weapons Coordination. Various colleagues of mine are concerning themselves in other directions. I'm merely filling in the general background for my own benefit. Woomera, the Minister's Liaison Section, Weapons Coordination—I want to establish their exact relationship and, in turn, how they tie in with Guildford and Research and Development."

"It's complicated," Lancaster said.

"A child's guide will do."

"All right."

He did his best not to confuse by oversimplification, giving the broad picture first, outlining the cumbersome apparatus of planning and action that followed Cabinet or ministerial decisions, then narrowing the picture down, concentrating on a typical weapon case history in order to illustrate as concisely as possible where departmental responsibilities began and ended. Sometimes he closed his eyes as he spoke as if he were dictating a long and involved memorandum. Now and again Sloan interjected a query, once in a while the cough racked him, but for the most part he was a model listener. Secrets were safe here, the room insulated by others, the walls thick enough to have spared

Lancaster complaints from neighbors when a party had occasionally got out of hand; yet he spoke quietly. What was ultimately at stake wasn't Sloan's direct concern. That knowledge meant power, or the diminution of another's power, wasn't a maxim that provided him with a *raison d'être.* "A rat-catcher," Gilligan had once described himself, and Sloan was no different. He might not look it, but he belonged to the same breed: the hunt was already on—discreetly, in confidence, beginning now in conversational tones to fumble toward whoever it was Adler's defection had exposed.

"Thank you," he said when Lancaster had finished. "You've been admirably clear." He drained his glass and put it down. "Now I'd like to turn to Weapons Coordination, if I may. What's the department's numerical strength?"

"Twenty-five."

"Including the director and deputy-director?"

"Twenty-five all told. McBride and Conway, three service section heads, each with a staff of two, a registrar, three male clerks, six secretaries, two copy-typists and a switchboard operator. She's blind, incidentally."

"And you."

"And me."

"All positive vetted, naturally." Sloan had this knack of making statements that somehow called for answers. "That goes without saying, of course."

"Yes, all PV cleared. And all periodically reviewed in the usual way."

"What exactly is your own position?"

"I'm the director's personal assistant."

McBride was bound to have mentioned this, yet Sloan went through the motions of asking. No stone personally

[ 44 ]

unturned, that was Sloan. And he also asked: "What additional responsibilities do you have, Mr. Lancaster?"

"Departmental security." An explanation seemed necessary. "I was with Inter-Services Security for a while so the job pretty well fell into my lap."

"I see." Sloan smiled. "Then I couldn't have been given a better contact, could I?" He would be polite to the last, Lancaster felt, right to the end, even if he were in at a killing. "I imagine you maintain personal data files on everyone in the department?"

"After a fashion."

Sloan raised his eyebrows slightly.

"Central Records have the ones that count." Lancaster shrugged. Sloan would know this, too; damned well he'd know it. "Ours are only second-best—age, grading, length of service, internal transfers; that kind of thing. They're very small change by comparison. Parochial."

"Nevertheless I'd like to look them over."

"They'll fill the best part of a suitcase."

"I suppose they will," Sloan agreed blandly, then changed tack, beginning to probe into office procedures, concentrating in particular on the method of progressing incoming and outgoing material. Again there wasn't always a short answer; many needed qualification. But after a while Lancaster did his best to sum up.

"We're on the receiving end from something over a dozen main sources, perhaps half of which channel in classified stuff. Naturally, everything of a classified nature is delivered by hand—plus a good deal that isn't. In fact I'd estimate that about eighty to ninety percent of all our traffic is by messenger and sealed bag. However, irrespective of the method of delivery, Dansie—he's our registrar—deals with it. He copes exclusively with receipt and subsequent distribution within the department, the circulation of all internal paper work, and also with outside despatch."

"What name did you say?" Sloan asked, coughing.

"Charles Dansie. He's our private post office—he and a male clerk . . . Pank," Lancaster added. "One-time Royal Marine sergeant."

"Have all the male clerks a service background?"

"Yes." Once more he found a pause drawing something extra out of him. "There's no cast-iron defense against leakage; there never was and never will be. The best that can be done is to limit circulation and access as much as possible, and this we do to extremes. For instance, originals of everything on the restricted list are held for reference in our strongroom—opening which is a two-key operation."

"Who has the keys?"

"Dansie one, Conway the other. In the absence of either, McBride or myself make ourselves responsible. Copies for internal consumption—we call them 'yellows'—are also deposited in the strongroom each evening. Section heads see to that, using locked boxes. And all yellows are destroyed as a matter of routine after forty-eight hours. Burned."

"By?"

"Pank. Under supervision, and after logging their return in his register." Lancaster leaned forward. "Short of chaining us to our desks and screwing everything down the system itself is about as watertight as you could expect."

"I'm sure," Sloan said, though that didn't mean he had done asking about it. The whiskey and the warmth of the fire seemed to be loosening his throat and bringing a very faint flush to his face; his eyes now had a glossy, slightly weepy, look. But his questions were as dogged as before. No, he wouldn't have another Scotch. No, thanks. . . . What interested him was how copies were made ("Xeroxed? I see. . . ."), by whom, and what checks there were on the numbers runoff. Presently he switched to night and weekend guard patrols in the building, then returned to various administrative details, some of them so petty that Lancaster wondered why he bothered. At times he could be tediously uninspired, bogged down in trivialities as if naïvely hopeful that they would lead him to some glaring flaw in the setup.

Then, quite suddenly, sensing perhaps that he was dredging an unproductive line, he changed tack again, reverting to Dansie and Pank. It was logical that he should do so; they were the hub around which the department revolved. Opportunity was concentrated there, and Sloan in his single-mindedness was merely focusing on the obvious. But Charles Dansie? Tommy Pank? The idea was preposterous, and Lancaster told Sloan as much.

"You're barking up the wrong tree with them. In fact, it's my view that you're barking up the wrong tree with Weapons Coordination as a whole."

"I hope you're right, Mr. Lancaster."

"I'm damn sure I'm right."

For the first and only time that evening Sloan's voice bore the merest trace of a bite. "I'd rather there was no misunderstanding between us. I appreciate how unpleasant this must be for you. But I haven't come remotely near a tree yet, let alone started barking." Off his own tongue the phrase seemed to cause him a certain grim amusement. "On the other hand you're in daily contact with twenty-four people who, to say the least, are in a privileged position."

Lancaster hesitated. "Look, ten times more than I could possibly tell you is on their files. And everything's available at Central Records—warts and all."

"When you're in the dark, Mr. Lancaster, it's surprising what can sometimes give you a sense of direction. And with security as part of your remit your views are of more than average interest."

"I don't recruit, nor am I in any way involved as a staff watchdog. If you imagine that, you're mistaken. I must have misled you. My security remit, as you put it, is almost entirely concerned with office procedures."

"Even so," Sloan said. More and more his cold was welling into his eyes; he dabbed them awkwardly. "Without going into detail I'd like you to fill me in a little with regard to your three service section heads."

"Owen, Navy; Hearne, Army; Baberton, Air Force." Lancaster reeled them off. "Since Roman Candle is an intended Army weapon it's a matter for Hearne's desk. And Stephen's as sound a person as you could find. They all are, all three. . . . Hell, what did you expect me to say?" Lancaster stood up irritably and refilled his glass. "What people do outside office hours, how they live, none of that's my concern. During hours, though, we're a team—a bloody good one."

"And Dansie?"

"What about him?"

"How long has he been with Weapons Coordination?"

"He was there when I joined. I couldn't say without checking."

"What sort of person is he?"

"Highly efficient."

"Pank?"

"First-rate. Bit of a plodder, but first-rate."

There was a break while Sloan coughed again. Then he said: "Are Owen and Baberton in any way involved with Roman Candle?"

"It's not their pigeon. As I told you, we limit circulation and access very rigorously."

"They know something about it, though?"

"In theory they shouldn't."

"In practice?" Sloan persisted.

"Possibly, but only on a hearsay level. No details. Not the kind of stuff Adler is said to have blown back."

"Who does have access then?"

"McBride, Conway, myself, Hearne and his two clerks, Dansie, Pank—and four secretaries."

"Whose secretaries?"

"McBride's, Conway's, Hearne's and my own."

Lancaster thought Sloan was going to ask about them, but he made one of his statements instead. "Which means twelve altogether—twelve, that is, officially aware of the details of this particular project."

"Officially, yes."

Sloan nodded, then looked at his watch as if coming to a decision with himself. He had been there nearly an hour.

Lancaster said: "But when you say 'officially' you're in danger of oversimplifying the position. As I pointed out earlier, no system's foolproof. You can't possibly be selective merely on the strength of what I've told you. If the department's suspect, everyone in it's suspect." He was beginning to argue like Conway.

"I'm excluding no one, Mr. Lancaster. I've merely been establishing certain elementary facts, and I'm more than grateful for your help." Sloan got to his feet rather stiffly, reluctant perhaps to face the waiting autumn chill. "I won't keep you any longer now. This has been very much in the nature of a preliminary. But I'll be in touch. Meanwhile I'd appreciate your letting me have those personal files at the earliest opportunity."

He gave his extension number at New Scotland Yard, then made for the door. In the hall, as he struggled into his raincoat, he said: "I may be wrong, but I've a feeling I've seen you somewhere before."

"It's possible. Though I'm told I've got one of those hotel-lobby sort of faces."

"When you were with Inter-Services Security perhaps?"

"Could be. I worked with one of your people then—Superintendent Gilligan."

Sloan frowned, almost there. "About three years ago? The Walker business?"

"That's right."

"The Walker business; yes, that must have been it." A thought seemed to hold him before he produced his version of a smile and held out a hand. "You'll know what it's all about then, Mr. Lancaster. . . . Good night, and thank you again. Don't bother. I'll see myself down."

He went with a cough and a sniff, and from the window

Lancaster watched him debouch into the street and disappear in the direction of the King's Road, presumably making for Hampstead, Hampstead and home and a mustard bath or whatever Mrs. Sloan, if there was one, reckoned was best. He hadn't exactly inspired confidence in his ability, but manner and appearance were no guide where Special Branch was concerned.

It was coming up to eight-thirty. Brooding, Lancaster took Linda's note from the mantelshelf. A bit of lust, a bit of curiosity, these had been enough until now. Linda had lasted longer than most, Linda with the blond hair and scarlet mouth who wore the bruises on her buttermilk skin like medals. Dismissively, he crumpled the note and dropped it into the waste-paper basket, then crossed the room and dialed Catherine's number.

"How are things in Holland Park?" he asked when she answered.

"Dreary."

"Here, too."

"You haven't got a mound of ironing waiting to be tackled, I bet."

"Can I come over a little later?"

She laughed softly. "You've put your lonely voice on, did you know?"

"It's the way I feel."

"Honestly, David, I'm up to my eyes." She paused. "Besides, you'd find it was a wasted journey."

"Oh," he said flatly.

"Could we eat somewhere tomorrow?"

"Tomorrow's a long way off."

"At Jerry's? I like it there."

"What do I do with myself until then?"

"Think about me."

"I'm beginning to do that without asking."

"All the time?"

"Nearly all."

"That's the nicest thing I've heard today." The sound of her indrawn breath suddenly traveled along the wire. "Oh hell . . . you probably won't believe me, but I've got something under the grill and it's burning."

"I'm dismissed, is that it?"

"Forgive me, darling. . . . Tomorrow, then—yes?"

Lancaster hung up, Sloan immediately filling his mind, Sloan and Adler, Conway and McBride. They were becoming an inescapable permutation. Conway would have had his session with Adler; an hour was all he'd wanted. Grimly, Lancaster finished the whisky he'd poured before Sloan left, then went into the kitchen and prepared himself a meal. Christ, yes, he knew what it was all about. The sands were running out for somebody. Openly he had defended the department, yet men like Sloan planted seeds. He sat at the table in the kitchen, munching reflectively, and if Catherine had been there she would have noticed the familiar tension. Later, he switched on the radio and mooched restlessly about, presently getting out his typewriter and writing a couple of letters. A little before ten he walked up to the King's Road and posted them, glad of the air and the excuse for a drink before closing time.

"Hallo," a brunette said to him in the saloon bar. "On your own, are you?" But he didn't need just anyone.

# Chapter 4 ] ✦

CONWAY buzzed him sharp on ten next morning, and even the double burr-burr somehow conveyed an implicit hostility.

"McBride asked me to brief you. Come now, would you?"

Sod it, Lancaster thought, this isn't a parade ground. Yet against his will he didn't delay. Catherine looked up in surprise when he entered her cramped outer office.

"D'you want to see him?"

"It's the other way round."

"Rather you than me. We're in a mood today." She raised her eyes to the ceiling.

"When weren't we?"

He touched her hand like a conspirator as he passed. Her perfume lingered as he pushed through into Conway's room, awakening a longing in him that was like a momentary foretaste of some as yet undiscovered pain. Conway was at his desk, plowing through a batch of yellows: deliberately he took his time. Apart from his in-tray the desk was as neat and polished as himself. Dansie, in a rare moment of pique, had once quoted him as an example of those for whom an obsessive orderliness was a substitute for sex. Lancaster had sat down, lit a cigarette and said "Well?" before the yellows were put carefully aside.

"It's about Adler."

"So I imagined."

"There's no doubt, absolutely no doubt, that the leak concerns Candle—that's the first thing. You were prepared to think otherwise, I know—"

"I *hoped* otherwise."

"—but from what Broom had told me earlier the writing was obviously on the wall. I'd have thought that was crystal clear yesterday." Conway shrugged meaningly. "However, Adler has since rewritten it in capital letters."

"To what extent?"

"Don't imagine he produced a verbal blueprint with every *i* dotted and every *t* crossed. I couldn't feed him. To be worth anything it had to come without clues from me. But, on several points, he was significantly accurate."

With impatience, Lancaster said: "Tell me."

"Guide system, for a start. Plus range capability and warhead characteristics."

"What else?"

"Isn't that enough?" Conway snapped.

"Power plant?"

"He was vague on that. And only barely on the mark with fuses. But he wasn't guessing. He was keen to prove his worth, more than keen, but even so he didn't overreach. Confined himself to facts—and mostly they fitted." Conway met and held Lancaster's gaze. "McBride's gone to inform the Minister. What happens next is up to him."

Lancaster showed no reaction. Dismay had hit him before the weekend and had since gone stale. Yesterday, with

Conway and the Old Man, the worst had been as good as confirmed. Conway was telling him nothing really new. It was clear, and had been clear for twenty-four hours, that the bottom had been ripped out of two years' work. What mattered now was how much could be saved.

Conway ran his hand over his pink face. "Here and there —on launching technique and control, for instance—Adler couldn't offer a thing. And, as I've said, he was vague about certain other details. All of which encourages me to believe that they haven't got the parcel completely wrapped up— not lock, stock and barrel . . . not yet, anyway. But a whale of a lot's gone."

"What about Discus?"

"Not a whisper. Not a whisper, thank God. He came clean, so with luck that's still intact." Conway stood up. "Have you seen Sloan?" he asked suddenly.

"Last night."

"What line's he taking?"

"Line? I couldn't say. Mainly he concentrated on how the department operates and where we fit in. I'll be giving Mc-Bride a full report."

Conway grunted, stung. He'd never approved of Lancaster's appointment, never accepted the idea of someone being in McBride's pocket, particularly a younger man. Dislike had been immediate, and mutual.

He started moving about the room, a habit of his, but Lancaster was damned if he was going to keep screwing his head around. "I might as well admit I don't much care for being put in the position of Special Branch informer. Sloan seems to be under the impression—"

"If you're so cast-iron sure that Weapons Coordination

is above suspicion I can't see what your objections are." Angrily, Conway fingered his pouter-pigeon tie. "When a twenty-million-pound weapon is found to have its back all but broken I don't even trust my nearest and dearest."

"You made that very clear yesterday." Lancaster couldn't decide what appalled Conway more, the waste or the betrayal. "I'm also repeating myself, but in case you've forgotten there *are* others involved. If you include the Woomera team there must be in the region of—"

"Adler's been fed on more than range-trials." Conway seemed nettled by Lancaster's dissatisfied shake of the head. "It's an elementary matter of putting two and two together. Take the suggested locking device on the stabilizers. That still belongs to the wind tunnel, yet our friend knew about it."

"All right," Lancaster conceded tartly. "All right. You saw him and I didn't. But we're still left with Guildford, Research and Development and the Liaison Section."

"Not if you continue to analyze the substance of the information."

"Adler isn't the horse's mouth."

"He's as near to it as we're likely to get. And if you jigsaw what he knows together you can make out a strong case for eliminating Guildford."

Lancaster said mockingly: "You're the one who ought to be liaising with Sloan. You'd have it all sewn up for him in no time." He stubbed his cigarette. "Hell, it was originally Guildford's baby. How can you so easily dismiss—"

"In certain respects, as you know, Guildford wouldn't any longer recognize their own child."

"So?"

"Adler did. Yes. And what goes for Guildford goes for Research and Development. For instance, they weren't involved with the warhead."

"Early on they were."

"Not with the later marks. Not with the cluster refinement."

"Adler had that?"

"In a nutshell." Conway said it almost with relish. "By my reckoning there are only two places where, overall, the cap could possibly fit—here and in the Liaison Section. Nowhere else is the thing handled in its entirety, performance data included."

Lancaster got to his feet. "You're beginning to sound as if the thought pleases you."

"I don't take your holier-than-thou attitude, if that's what you mean. Candle's in jeopardy, and more besides. I don't give a tuppenny damn where the leak is so long as it's plugged and the bastard goes to the wall. And if you find my basic deduction unpalatable, all I can say is that Special Branch are hardly likely to."

Lancaster clenched his hands. Only with difficulty did he refrain from pettiness. "You'd like to narrow the possibilities down even more, wouldn't you? You'd like the source to be here, right under our noses, so that the outcry accelerates the Old Man's going." But he managed to hold his tongue. Conway was enemy enough, the future uncertain enough, as it was. He went to the door without another word and let himself into Catherine's room.

One glance at his face was sufficient to make her say: "I warned you, didn't I now?"

He was trembling very slightly. There wasn't a part of

her he didn't know and didn't want, not a smile he didn't wish to match, not a glance he didn't want to hold. But he couldn't switch from Conway as if nothing had happened. He swore quietly, caught up again in the turmoil of what was at stake, tongue-tied by a secrecy she didn't share.

"I'm sorry about last night, David."

"That's all right."

"What time at Jerry's? Eight?"

He seemed to come back from a long way away. "Eight?" Then his features softened fractionally. "Eight. Yes. That'll be fine."

She blew him a kiss as he left. Tyndall, Hearne's senior clerk, walked heavily past him in the cream-distempered corridor, files in hand. "Morning, Mr. Lancaster"—and Sloan surfaced at once, Sloan with his early attempt at a likely short-list.

"Morning, Bob."

Tyndall? Automatically the question mark insisted; this was going to keep happening now. Tyndall? Hardly. . . . And there were others in what Sloan had termed a privileged position whom it was farcical even to contemplate. The Old Man, for one. Conway too, damn him. And Catherine. . . . She at least was safe, come what may.

McBride had him in later during the morning. "Ah, David," he began. "I understand George has had a word with you."

"Yes."

"I've never seen the Minister so furious. He's been hoping against hope like the rest of us, I suppose. But anger doesn't help—not that I could tell him so." He tapped his fingertips together, lips pursed, nostrils a little flared as if a wound had broken and at last he could smell its sepsis. "It's bad, David. Very, very bad. If there's any consolation it's in Adler having come across when he did. At least we now have a chance to stop the rot. . . . You've had a preliminary session with Sloan?"

"He spent an hour with me last evening."

"What did you make of him?"

"It's early to say. He was in the throes of a cold, so I suppose I didn't see him at his sharpest. But he didn't miss much. I gave him an explanation of our function and the way in which we operate internally, after which we got on to a rundown of the staff. He wants me to let him have the personal files."

"Our own?"

Lancaster nodded.

"I can't see what use they'll be to him."

"Neither can I."

"The kind of lead he's looking for is never in the records. God knows what corrupts a person, but it won't be logged in a file—that's a certainty." McBride narrowed his eyes as if he were resurrecting a memory. "However, I'm sure Sloan has a reason for what he's doing. Special Branch aren't exactly fools, David."

"He was also keen to establish who has what he called 'maximum opportunity' insofar as Roman Candle's concerned."

"How many did you say?"

"Twelve."

"As many as that, is it?"

"Including you and Conway, yes."

The Old Man rubbed the bridge of his nose while Lancaster added the other names. So little appears on the face when the will is in control. McBride was silent for a while, and when he spoke it was as if he were thinking aloud. "It's an ugly business, suddenly to be forced into questioning the fidelity of one's colleagues."

With more venom than he realized, Lancaster said: "Conway's already discarded Guildford, Woomera, and Research and Development."

"Logically, I thought." McBride glanced at him with pale gray eyes. "Didn't you?"

"I'm not entirely convinced."

"Or is it that you don't want to be? The reasoning's sound, you know. But it's only human nature to disbelieve where the signs might be pointing. For my part I've always thought of Weapons Coordination—how shall I say?—as being like Caesar's wife. And I daresay the Minister has reacted in self-same fashion—that his own Liaison Section couldn't possibly harbor a traitor." His red telephone rang but he delayed before answering it. "When d'you see Sloan again?"

"At lunchtime."

"I expect to be kept informed, remember."

"Yes, sir. Incidentally, I'll be at the testing ground tomorrow. They're setting up the P-Five fuse."

McBride nodded, but Lancaster wasn't quite sure whether he'd heard or not. For a moment he felt almost sorry for him: that knighthood in the Old Man's briefcase was in danger of vanishing.

Margaret's lunch hour was between one and two, though frequently she stretched it. Hair appointment, shopping for an invalid mother—there was always a reason. Lancaster waited for her to go before unlocking the personal cabinet and extracting the files. Some of them he glanced through, his own included. Place of birth, date of birth, next of kin, schools, university, marital status, previous departments and positions held, current position, date of Positive Vetting, date of subsequent clearance . . . That kind of information branded no one, hinted at no one. When they closed Walker's file Colonel Gray had written in the margin: *This man excelled in all the things that make the human race so dubious an experiment.* But that was being wise after the event, which was Gray's forte.

He had brought a Revelation from the flat and now he packed the twenty-five folders into it. The key to the cabinet was his responsibility, so he could always fob Margaret off if she needed it to be opened. "Between these four walls, David . . ." All right, but it meant playing games.

Dansie joined him in the lift. The suitcase caught his eye. "Off on leave somewhere?"

"Wish I were."

Nothing more was said. Dansie inclined to keep himself amiably to himself, blinking away behind rimless spectacles. He was middle-aged now, yet he still retained his scrum-half figure. Fourteen England caps, a cracking war record, private money—again Lancaster found himself making superficial assessments. "Beware of everyone," McBride had once told him. "Most of all beware of those who parade their weaknesses." But it was hard to imagine that even a hidden flaw existed in Dansie's makeup. He seemed the soundest person possible, the least worth wondering about.

Lancaster took a taxi to New Scotland Yard. He had telephoned Sloan earlier in the day and fixed a one-thirty appointment. But when he was shown up to Sloan's office a youngish, brick-complexioned man in a gray suit explained that Sloan had succumbed to his cold and gone home.

"He was pretty groggy when he arrived, and it was getting the better of him all the time, so he pushed off about midday. Best thing, really."

"Does that mean I have to lug this case back where I brought it from?"

"Oh no. The Superintendent told me to make sure you left it." He noticed Lancaster's hesitation and added: "I'm Superintendent Sloan's assistant. These are the Weapons Coordination files, aren't they?"

Lancaster nodded. "You'll need the keys." He fished them out and parted with them. "In view of the Superintendent being off sick, how long will it be before I can have everything back?"

"Tomorrow?"

"I won't be available tomorrow."

"Thursday, then? It's merely a question of checking what's here with Central Records. Discrepancies sometimes exist, and they're always worth looking into."

So that was it: every-avenue Sloan. "Let's make it Thursday. I'll call for them at the same time."

"Very well, Mr. Lancaster."

He returned on foot along Whitehall and ate a cold lunch in a pub near Trafalgar Square. A woman on the stool next to his at the counter was reading an early edition of the *Evening News* and, like something addressed to Lancaster alone, Adler's name leaped at him from a typewriter advertisement.

There could be no escape from the consequences of Adler now. And if Conway's argument proved contagious, Weapons Coordination would soon be virtually under siege, the hunt no longer at arm's length. Personal loyalties didn't exist when the net began to close: Walker had once been a colleague of sorts. You hunted with the rest, from the inside. Sentiment became a word, pity a word.

Yet a latent part of him had been aroused, tempted. Involuntarily he'd found entrance to a woman's heart and the temptation was to wonder if he could climb in and somehow shut out the world. Peace of mind was suddenly desirable; peace of mind and permanence. Instead of which he was committed to a situation that made him different from everyone who now shared the counter with him, oblivious in their prosperous contentment of the enormity of what was at risk.

By twenty past two he was back at his desk. On the ground floor and again on the fifth he had shown his pass. It was daily routine, yet at times like these even the familiar could seem to be riddled with significance, as if, already, Weapons Coordination had been set specially apart.

Stephen Hearne sauntered into his office as the afternoon was dying. He tapped on the glass of Margaret's cubicle, flashing her a smile as he crossed toward Lancaster.

"Question number one."

"Shoot."

"Where have all the yellows gone?" he asked lightly. "Long time passing."

"I hadn't noticed."

"Then you're either blind or—what I've privately suspected for ages—not giving the job your wholehearted attention." He grinned, high white collar nestling into the curly neck hair. "Seriously, who's sitting on them?"

"No one, to my knowledge. I initialed some this morning."

"Oh, I saw that lot, but you could have rolled a cigarette with 'em. Guildford seems to have gone completely out of business, Research and Development ditto."

"Didn't strike me, I must say." Without effort Lancaster warded him off. "What's question number two?"

"Are we playing squash tomorrow?"

"No."

"Wow. Ask a straight question and you get a straight answer. Any good reason?"

"I'll be wallowing ankle-deep in mud on the testing ground for most of the day, that's why."

"You're getting soft."

"The Brigadier walked me into the ground last time, and I'm not taking you on in the condition I was then."

"What's on the program, the P-Five?"

Lancaster nodded. "The Old Man asked me to stand in for him. And you know what it's like trying to get away from there once the postmortems start. . . . Can we make it tomorrow week?"

"Sure."

"Sorry. I should have let you know."

"Can't be helped. I expect Nadine will drag me out to some film or other instead, so she'll bless you for the opportunity."

"How is Nadine?"

"In very good nick, considering. Bit unsettled after her jaunt back home to Brussels, but otherwise fine. Blooming, you could say. . . ." Hearne could never quite succeed in glossing over the state of his marriage. The smile, the cheerful casualness, the easy gestures—the veneer was very thin where Nadine was concerned. "Well, this won't set the Thames on fire. 'Bye, David." On the way out he turned. "Let me know if the P-Five works or whether it blows half the technology-of-death boys to kingdom come."

"Which would you prefer?"

"As long as you're spared, matey, I think I probably wouldn't weep over the latter. It would make quite a change, wouldn't it?"

"So it would if a new fuse functioned first time. . . . 'Bye."

Jerry's was on the northern fringe of Soho. There were smarter places, brighter places, but the food and service was good, the atmosphere friendly. Lancaster arrived just before eight; he hadn't booked a table, but Mario found him one.

"There, Mr. Lancaster, how's that? An aperitif while you're waiting?"

"A Scotch. Scotch and water."

He lit a cigarette and glanced about him as if idly in search of friends, but Mario and some of the waiters provided the only familiar faces. He didn't see Catherine arrive; the first he was aware of her being there was when she said "Hallo" from a few feet away.

"You must have a private trap door."

"Have you been here long?"

"Only a minute or two."

His whiskey came and Catherine asked for a Campari. She wore a tight-fitting avocado-colored dress with a low back. No rings, no bracelets, no lipstick, no mascara: a pearl necklace was her only concession, and the effect was stunning. Smooth black hair, marvelously white arms and shoulders.

"You're a dream," he said.

"It's lovely to see you smile."

"Is that so unusual?"

"You were hardly smiling this morning."

"Conway brings out the worst in me. Anyhow, don't let's go on to him, for Pete's sake."

It was hard to believe that her file was possibly under scrutiny at that very moment. Special Branch didn't keep office hours, and Sloan wasn't a one-man band; there was a team in the background. But they'd have to scratch a sight deeper, and more urgently, than that.

He took Catherine's hand and the contact was like balm. He was restless, but he couldn't let it show. Denials, protestations, he wanted to be spared any need for those: they would only drag his thoughts back to the treadmill and the one thing that gagged him.

"Did you phone your father last night?"

She nodded.

"All well?"

"Aches and pains, but nothing out of the ordinary."

She telephoned Evesham faithfully every Monday at nine. Twice in the half-year he'd known her she had traveled west to spend a weekend there. Her mother had remarried and she rarely mentioned her; in New Zealand—Auckland, was it?—she had a sister. This was about the limit of his knowledge of her family, though there was a bond between her and her father that he sometimes envied. Families belonged to other people. His own father and mother were dead and there never were any brothers or sisters; only an uncle who unfailingly sent him a Christmas card from an address in Stirling. His parents had died in a car crash when he was twenty, and the following year seemed to have been spent mostly in fighting for compensation in the courts. He was denied it in the end because of an ingenious technicality, but the estate left him with something—not much, but enough. So there was no hardship; he was never poor, never hungry.

Catherine sipped her Campari. "By the way—one piece of shop. Only one, I promise. I think you'll find McBride will be pulling out at the end of the year."

The line of his mouth tightened fractionally. "Oh?"

She nodded.

"Are you sure?"

"He implied as much when he was in with Conway this afternoon."

"What did he say?"

"I only got the tail end of it, but it was something about something not being his baby after December."

"'Something about something'?" Despite himself, Lancaster's lips curled. "A fine undercover woman you'd make."

"I was barely through the door. Anyhow it wasn't so much what he said as the way he said it."

He could chuckle now, veins showing in his temples. "You're a marvel."

"Has he mentioned it to you?"

"No. It's been on the cards, though I hadn't imagined it would come about quite so soon."

"His actual words were that he wanted to get 'this business' finished while the responsibility was still his. If that doesn't suggest—"

" 'This business'?"

"Quote 'this business' unquote. And Conway changed the subject when he saw I was there."

"I'll have to nominate you for the Detective of the Year award."

"You're a small-minded, patronizing so-and-so." Catherine squeezed his hand gently. "What will happen when McBride goes?"

He raised his shoulders, let them drop. "Conway expects the Minister will do his duty."

"You'll never last a week with Conway." Her huge blue eyes were serious, concerned.

"Maybe I will, maybe I won't."

"He'll have you out as soon as he can."

"Maybe."

"Doesn't it worry you?"

"Next time I wake and find it's two o'clock in the morning, then it will worry me. But not now." He signaled Mario. "Right now I'm starving and you're starving, so we're going to order and then we're going to talk about something entirely different."

"Such as?"

"You, for instance."

Perhaps it was because he knew he wouldn't be making love to her that he seemed to need her more. He had come a long way with her since their first meeting and that unaccustomed rebuff. Again, as they ate and their conversation ebbed and flowed, the future intruded on Lancaster, niggling at the edges of his mind. Catherine was right; he'd never survive under Conway. McBride made many things possible, allowed him scope, trusted him; and trust was the most important factor of all. With Conway he would be living from day to day, hamstrung, his usefulness impaired.

He looked at Catherine, alarmed within his uneasiness by the crisis she knew nothing of, the names she knew nothing of—Adler's, Sloan's . . . and that other name that no one knew. Her face was beautiful to watch, calm, hinting at an inner tranquillity that he wished could be his instead of the hard core of anxiety that seemed to have become almost a part of his physical self.

Conway could wait, though. Conway was a warning light on the horizon. What was to be the Old Man's swan song dominated everything else: first things first. Something squalid was on the way.

Later, as their taxi headed for Holland Park, he said: "I won't see you tomorrow. I'll be down at the testing ground and haven't a clue what time I'll get back." Oxford Street flashed and winked at them, people's faces green under the neon. "But will you come to Kilvarna again this weekend?"

"Of course."

"You'd really like to?"

"On one condition."

"What is it?"

"That you won't wag a superior finger at me next time I say I love you."

"Did I do that?"

"You did indeed."

"Well, I won't again."

"Never?"

"Never."

He put an arm around her shoulders, drawing her close, and there wasn't even a hint of interrogation in her kiss.

# Chapter 5 ] ✦

**A** CHILL breeze moved fitfully across the scarred expanses of gorse and heather.

"Weapons Coordination? Thank you, sir."

The corporal saluted with parade-ground violence before lifting the barrier, but Lancaster had no illusions; it must have been the devil's own job to keep warm and not many vehicles would be coming through.

He could see four up at the assembly point: staff car, Land Rover, a couple of jeeps. There was a hut just below the crest of a longish slope, backed by a clump of pines, and a rutted track determined the route to take. The ruts were deep and, because of its clearance, he took the Triumph Spitfire gingerly in second.

"All right on the roads, those things," the Brigadier said as Lancaster swung in beside the hut. "All right there. Useless in a place like this." He'd made the self-same remark last time they'd met. "Cold?"

"I've been warmer."

"Had breakfast?"

"Three hours ago. I could do with some tea, though."

"Got it waiting for you. Come on inside."

"Am I the last?"

"Except for Norris. Anyhow, not to worry, we've time in hand. It isn't nine yet."

The hut was bare and the clatter of their feet bounced off the walls. Opposite the door was a trestle table with a battered urn on it, cups and saucers, a bottle of milk and a packet of sugar. Lancaster helped himself. Peterson, of Experimental Weapons, was already there together with the morose-looking range master and two of his control party.

"Morning," Peterson grunted. "D'you think the rain will hold off?"

"Too breezy for rain, I'd have thought."

"A sure sign you're no country man," the Brigadier laughed.

"I'm not," Lancaster said easily. "I'm a chairborn urban troglodyte, but I cling to the old wives' tales of my youth. Do you reckon it'll rain, then?"

"No," the Brigadier said. "No, I don't actually."

He had the palest blue eyes Lancaster had ever seen and was as lean as a whippet, the tanned skin stretched tight over the bones. He kept moving his feet as though he wanted to relieve himself. "Come on," he muttered every now and then, peering through the door down the long track to the road, "come on, Norris." The range master and the two with him didn't utter a word, either between themselves or to anybody else, and Peterson had evidently decided that one question was enough.

"Got some gumboots in the jeep if you want 'em," the Brigadier presently said to Lancaster.

"Thanks."

They went outside. "Damned moody lot in there this morning," the Brigadier complained. "Think we were at a funeral or something. . . . Ah, there's Norris now." The car was all of a quarter of a mile away but he cupped his hands and bawled: "Hurry it up, man. Day's nearly gone."

Norris was from the Liaison Section. The car lurched up the track like a buffalo. "Sorry," Norris said with a disarming smile as he clambered out. "Was I keeping you?"

"Not really. How about some tea?"

"No, thanks. . . . Hallo, Lancaster." Norris was a compulsive hand-shaker. "Got your fingers crossed?"

"Toes as well."

"Right you are, gentlemen," the Brigadier called into the hut. "We're ready when you are."

Norris and Peterson climbed into one of the jeeps, Lancaster and the Brigadier into the other. The control party used the Land Rover and set off in the lead. There was no sun, a lot of pewter-colored cloud; the breeze stung Lancaster's face as the convoy rumbled over the crest and dipped down the reverse slope. Norris was in the jeep in front. Did he know? Lancaster wondered. Almost certainly not. If the Minister had confided in anyone it would be Wakeling, the Liaison Section's head. Norris was a technical interpreter for ministerial minds; a good one, very good, but no more, no less. Even so he'd be on Sloan's opposite number's list of possibles—whether he knew or not. Nobody was better briefed on Roman Candle than Norris.

They covered about a mile. It was a roller coaster of a track. "First-rate for a liver," the Brigadier exclaimed cheerfully when a particularly atrocious bump lifted them off their seats. He would go mad, Lancaster thought, if ever he was posted to the confines of Whitehall. They followed the Land Rover around the soggy rim of a pond, took a left-hand fork in the ruts and reached a more level stretch. Red marker flags flapped like abandoned battle standards amid the wastes of scrub; tank treads patterned bare patches. "Rigged up a new simulated homing gadget," the Brigadier grunted. "Trolley on a length of rail. Hell of a sight better than all those blasted wires."

Lancaster glimpsed a three-tonner in the depression ahead, but not much else. A plantation of conifers screened most of the site from the track and he had to wait until they had snaked their way down to the floor of the depression before he could see the changes that had been made since last month. The web of overhead wires was still there, criss-crossing above the target tower: until now they'd homed the fuses along the wires from varying angles.

"Well, what d'you think?" the Brigadier asked as he switched off. "More like it, eh?"

Four lengths of narrow-gauge rail extended at right angles from the squat tower; each was about one hundred yards long, and from fifty yards the distance to the tower was measured off in feet. There was only one trolley and it carried what looked like a miniature open-ended Nissen hut mounted on its low platform. Thick black rubber was bonded to the running surface of the wheels. Sand-bagged buffers protected the base of the tower.

"How's it controlled?" Lancaster asked.

"Electrically, from the three-tonner."

"How d'you get it onto one of the other sets of rails?"

"Have to manhandle it. Nuisance, that. Really we need four of 'em, but we're up against the Treasury as usual. However, it's not a bad little toy. Come and see."

They left the jeep. Norris and Peterson were already walk-

ing across to the trolley, accompanied by the range master.
Four or five men in denims were standing by the three-
tonner and one of them detached himself from the group,
coming at an easy trot to join the Brigadier. He was new to
Lancaster; a REME sergeant with the build of a middle-
weight.

"Morning, sir."

"Morning, sergeant. All set?"

"Sir."

"Is the thing going to work?"

"No reason why it shouldn't, sir."

"Good." The Brigadier turned to the range master. "Better
if you took over now, John. You're the boss."

"Well, gentlemen, a few words first about the trolley itself. We can move it in toward the tower at any speed we
choose between a slow crawl and about forty m.p.h.—slow,
quick, and at the double." The voice was as lugubrious as the
expression. "The cable-link with the truck not only allows
us to drive the trolley but it also sends back the exact point
at which fuse reaction occurs. There's a visual aid alongside
the rails, as you see, which is quite adequate for very low-
speed operation. I daresay the whole thing looks a bit Heath
Robinson, but I think you'll agree when you've seen it in
operation that it's an improvement on the wires. Now"—he
heaved himself onto the trolley's platform and put a hand
on the heavy steel Nissen-like roof—"under the hood here
there's really no change. Insulation's the same, mounting's
the same, temperature control ditto. We've merely got rather
more space." The breeze fluttered stray ends of dark hair
around the rim of his beret. "I thought we'd give the trolley
a demonstration run before loading and getting down to

serious business." He glanced at the Brigadier. "Right, sir?"

"Right by me—unless, that is, there are any questions. . . . No? Fine. Give us a few minutes to get the transport out of harm's way, then it's all yours, John."

Everyone except Norris and Lancaster moved off. "How's McBride?" Norris asked. "In good form?"

"Very."

"Haven't seen him for quite some time." He could have been fishing. "And Conway? On the ball as usual?"

"Oh, yes."

Norris indicated the trolley. "More do-it-yourself kit. Makes one wonder if our lords and masters will ever get off their penny-farthings and stop expecting miracles." He sounded amused. "Cigarette?"

"Not just now, thanks."

The jeeps and the Land Rover were grumbling in the direction of the three-tonner. The cold breeze came in snatches, blowing from the east over the undulating plain, making the heather sway. You never saw any birds here; intermittent explosions had long since scared them off, instinct warning them to keep permanently away: quiet could deceive.

Norris tucked his head into his right shoulder to shelter the flame of his lighter. The confidential attitude was unintentional; there wasn't anyone within a hundred yards. "How d'you feel about the P-Five being under consideration for Roman Candle?"

"For Discus."

"For Roman Candle as well."

"That's news."

Smoke streamed as the cigarette caught. "Woomera had some late reservations on Candle's last firing with regard to fuse effectiveness." Norris might have been drafting one of his reports. He frowned, surprised. "Surely you knew that?" And then, because there was a pause: "Weapons Coordination must be slipping."

"There's so much stuff coming through that you need six pairs of eyes and a memory like a computer."

"It was sometime last week. Early on."

"A Round Robin?"

"Yes."

"Then you've caught me out. I must have missed it." Puzzled, Lancaster stared into the distance.

"I hoped we were through with any more modifications on Candle, I must say. The trouble with some people is that they can't leave well alone. Candle ought to have been in production months ago, but what with the stabilizers and the umpteenth-mark nose cone and now the possibility of switching to the P-Five it'll be this time next year before it's operational." Norris brushed a strand of tobacco from his lower lip. "Small wonder half the stomachs in the Liaison Section are barnacled with ulcers." He gestured enviously toward the three-tonner. "Look at 'em. As far as Peterson and the Brigadier and the rest are concerned this is just another proximity job that may or may not work. Marvelous, isn't it? The less you know I reckon the easier you sleep and the longer you live."

They started moving to join the others, Lancaster thinking, mystified. Try as he might he couldn't recall that particular Round Robin.

"Better stretch out, I suppose," Norris said, "otherwise we'll be in the doghouse. And I've been last once today already."

"Right, gentlemen," the range master shouted above the din of the generator in the back of the three-tonner. "This is a dry run, remember."

They were all in a bunch, collars up, sixty or seventy paces from the trolley. The cable-link was loosely coiled on the ground, ready to unwind. Two men in denims were huddled with the generator and the dials under the truck's canvas top and the sergeant squatted on the tailboard.

"Ready, sergeant?"

"Sir."

"Let her go, then. Speed her up toward the finish."

The noise of the generator intensified abruptly and the trolley began to move forward. It went at about walking speed for half the length of rail, then suddenly accelerated; it was doing perhaps twenty miles an hour by the time it thudded into the buffers below the tower. Four members of the control party sprinted over and wheeled it back to the far end of the track, recoiling the cable as they did so.

"We'll just demonstrate that once again," the range master shouted. "At an absolute crawl to begin with, then as fast as she can shift."

There was an almighty crunch when the trolley hit the buffers. Dust erupted; some of the sandbags collapsed.

"Not to worry," was the Brigadier's comment. "No damage done. Have to expect minor teething troubles with a gadget like this. It functions, that's the main thing."

"God in heaven," Norris muttered close to Lancaster.

"You see, gentlemen," the range master shouted at them, "we can virtually inch her forward or really push her through like a dose of salts." He seemed almost elated.

Why they had to stand so close to the truck, Lancaster couldn't understand. "Good idea," the Brigadier agreed when he mentioned it. "Let's move away a bit. Can't hear ourselves think here. What's next on the agenda, John? Are you running the real thing this time?"

"Yes, sir."

"Very well. This is where you come into your own, Peterson."

They hung about for a quarter of an hour or more while Peterson supervised loading the fuse. Lancaster and Norris watched to begin with, but there wasn't much to be learned from watching; shielded by a hinged lid the fuse was set in the center of a tulip-shaped porcelain tube under the front of the trolley's hood. In the past they'd suspended fuses from the wires and homed them like cable cars. It had gone ten before preparations were completed and the obligatory warning flag was run up on the tower. Somewhere above the roof of cloud an aircraft was droning over.

Where they were standing now the range master could speak without bawling at them as if they were recruits. "We're going to nose the trolley in at slow speed, four to five miles an hour. The critical point should be around the hundred-and-fifty-foot mark. . . . Get her going, sergeant."

The trolley traveled silently on its rubberized wheels. Everyone was very quiet, like the time when the electric hare nears the traps. Nothing was expected to happen over the first half of its journey, and nothing did. But nothing happened when the trolley reached the beginning of the distance scale and nothing happened all the way along to the tower's base. The run was a total failure. No reaction, nothing. Peterson was swearing well before the trolley clinked against the buffers.

"Cut the power, sergeant!"

"Well?" the Brigadier asked of no one in particular. "What's to be made of that?"

Peterson's glance contained hatred. He set off heavily toward the trolley, poked his head under the hood when he got there and dickered about for a minute or two before starting back with the Brigadier, who had joined him.

"Peterson thought the shield might not have lifted."

"Had it?" This was Norris.

"Yes," Peterson said, "it bloody well had."

"Come on, John," the Brigadier called briskly to the range master. "Let's try her again. . . . Teething troubles, gentlemen," he said, blowing on his hands. "Teething troubles."

The control party hauled the trolley along the rails and relooped the cable. The breeze seemed colder now, blowing more steadily; the square warning flag was as stiff as if it had been starched.

"All set? Take her away, sergeant."

The trolley trundled gently along its hundred-yard run and came to rest against the buffers.

"Could it be the alignment?" Norris suggested.

"Doubt it," Peterson fumed. "Oh bugger the blasted thing."

He went off once more, raging, and Norris went with him. The Brigadier remained with Lancaster; he looked slightly bewildered. "Odd," he said at least twice. "Damned odd, this."

They ran the trolley six times more—three times at half speed, three times flat out—with the same exasperating, negative result. It was an exposed place in which to put one's patience to the test. On the sixth run the trolley was derailed and the control party took ten minutes to right it and restack the sandbags.

Pink-nosed with cold, Norris looked at Lancaster. He wasn't amused any more. "It's enough to make one weep. What was wrong with the wires? I didn't come down to watch people playing trains."

The Brigadier heard him. "I don't think a remark like that's justified, Norris."

"Well, I do. This morning's been an out-and-out waste of everybody's time."

"I wouldn't say that. I wouldn't say that at all." The Brigadier never seemed quite sure of himself with civilians; it was as if he needed the evidence of a badge of rank to know exactly where he stood. Civilians were tricky in that respect, particularly one with a Minister close behind him. "Practice makes perfect. And like everybody else we're in the hands of the budget boys. We have to scrimp and make do. I think John and his fellows have done a damned fine job in the circumstances."

Lancaster said: "The P-Five seems like a dead loss, anyhow."

"That's too pessimistic a view, in my opinion. Pessimistic and premature." The Brigadier shifted his weight back and forth, his lean face like a Victorian depiction of hope and fortitude. "Let's go see what Peterson makes of everything."

Peterson was crouched by the trolley's hood, rubbing the

porcelain casing of the fuse as if he were attempting to revive a corpse.

"Any conclusions, Peterson?"

"No," Peterson said icily. "Except that I think this is a cockeyed setup."

"I was asking about the fuse. Shall we try another run?"

"What's the time?"

"Eleven-fifty."

"All right. But if there's no response I want to see what happens using the other set of rails."

"Any particular reason?"

"Because they're there, for one thing."

"A change of direction might help, is that it?" the Brigadier suggested defensively.

"God knows. But it's worth a try."

Everyone moved clear and waited for the range master's order. When it came the trolley rolled slow-speed toward the buffers and finally bumped to a standstill; that was all.

"Cut it!"

There was a moment's silence before the sergeant's voice came on the breeze.

"We've got ourselves a real reluctant virgin with us today, lads. A real sluggish little back-room boy of a virgin."

Then another voice: "Make up your mind, sergeant." And raucous laughter.

"I suggest we go and lick our wounds over lunch, gentlemen," the Brigadier said.

Three of them went with him—Norris, Peterson and Lancaster. They went in one of the jeeps, the Brigadier at the wheel, and as usual he drove them to the Grenadier, a small mock-Tudor roadside pub a mile or so outside the prohibited area. They warmed themselves with whisky at the bar before taking the *table d'hôte* meal. "Don't like to nag," the Brigadier said when refusing a second round, "but we ought to be back sharp on one-thirty. Only fair on the men." He would have been happier in bivouac.

They ate with bottle-glass windows alongside and black beams above. The morning's fiasco was only spasmodically referred to, as if everyone were tacitly agreed that discussion would solve nothing. Other people were too close, anyhow. The most Peterson would say was: "It had a clean bill at Guildford. One hundred percent, with fuse response within very narrow tolerances. To be honest I haven't a clue."

"Temperature?" Norris offered. "Could that be a factor?"

"Hardly."

"Vibration? After all, that wretched trolley—"

But Peterson was shaking his head. And the Brigadier said: "The trolley's a sight better than what we had previously—frozen wires, jammed capsules. You forget, Norris."

"Far from it." Norris never knew when to stop. It was always the same down here when things went wrong. Bicker, bicker. If it wasn't him it was someone else. Now he said: "Sometimes I think Gilbert and Sullivan were born a century too early."

Lancaster kept out of it. They drove back to the testing ground, arriving promptly at the half hour. The trolley had been man-handled to the rails lying at ninety degrees from the track they'd used all morning and the three-tonner had been shifted around to allow the cable full play. Just before two o'clock the trolley made its first run and the fuse reacted almost at the beginning of the distance scale. A cheer went up.

"Hundred and forty-two feet, five inches," the sergeant called from the truck.

Elated, Peterson charged off through the scrub, the Brigadier excitedly after him. "That's more like it, Peterson, eh?"

The trolley was reloaded and put through another run. Flame and dust enveloped it at approximately the same point. The explosion was as sharp as a cracking whip and the disused overhead wires quivered as if they'd been plucked.

"Hundred and forty-one, eight," the sergeant bawled after verification.

The Brigadier couldn't resist a dig: "What d'you say to that, Norris?"

"Why the hell's it functioning now?" Norris wanted to know. "Merely because of a change of approach? If so, what's that supposed to tell us?"

Peterson had the trolley brought back to the first track. It all took time and the breeze was as chilling as before. Three homing runs were made and, as before, all were unsuccessful. There was no obvious explanation. They tried each of the stretches of rail in turn. On two—those lying roughly north to south—there were no failures and fuse reaction was always between 144 and 138 feet. On the third track there was reaction twice out of five runs at roughly 120 feet. But the original track continued to draw a blank.

Mystified, though not despondent, Peterson eventually agreed to call it a day. The light was already murky. They returned in convoy to the hut and drank hot tea, stamping their feet to get the circulation going, openly discussing the baffling features of the test, without rancor now. It was nearly six before they broke up and went their separate ways. Lancaster was the first to leave. "Mind how you go in that thing," the Brigadier said as the Spitfire started to move. "Not really the kind of transport you need for ground like this, you know."

The traffic thickened over the last homeward hour or so, forcing Lancaster to cut his speed. He dined at Esher on his way back to Chelsea. In the hut Norris had said to him privately: "I'd say that puts paid to any idea of the P-Five for Candle, wouldn't you? Time's not so pressing for Discus. But this one for Candle?" He'd blown a raspberry and left it at that.

Lancaster arrived at his flat a little after ten. Day-long exposure to the biting weather had left him with a throb of weariness. He dialed Catherine's number shortly after getting home, but there was no answer and he felt a small dull ache of resentment that others might have some claim on her time. Later he wrote some notes on the P-Five. It was contrary to security ever to commit oneself officially to paper outside the office or to carry documents on one's person, but Lancaster was careful to jot down only what might otherwise slip his mind and which, unrelated to anything specific, was harmless enough—merely the number of runs and the number of successes in each direction with the approximate reaction distances. Underneath he added proposed use and a series of interrogation marks, then locked the sheet of paper away in the bureau.

He tried Catherine's number once again before turning in. There was more to preoccupy him than the way the test had gone, more than an apparent slipup over a Round Robin. Sloan was always intruding—on the drive home, during the day, at dinner. Increasingly Lancaster kept putting himself in Sloan's shoes, casting endlessly about for a likely weak link. It was impossible not to, impossible to be privy to the situation and wait for someone else to make the moves. Gilligan had finally nailed his man, but not without help, not without a lead. "You're hard underneath," Catherine had told him once. "Deep down I believe you're as hard as stone. Honestly—I'm not joking. I can't see you ever finding yourself in tears."

He thought of her now as fatigue began to best him, and for a while she went with him into his sleep. But not for long. Someone else was soon there, someone in a dirty trenchcoat, a stranger, someone he'd never seen before in his life and saw only vaguely now. "Mr. Lancaster?" this man said in the blur. "My name's Adler. Perhaps you've heard of me?"

He gave McBride a verbal account of the P-Five test next morning. Norris would précis Peterson's report, of course, and a copy would be circulated within a few days, but the Old Man wouldn't be content to remain in the dark until that happened. He was to have been there himself, anyhow. Lancaster gave him the gist of what he'd noted down at home, plus a description of the new layout and its shortcomings.

McBride said: "It doesn't sound too encouraging."

"No, sir."

"Peterson was most optimistic about the P-Five, I know."

"I think myself it was a pity they chose to use it as

a guinea pig. Still, I'd say it's some way from being ready. Whatever the reason, on yesterday's showing it's erratic and unpredictable."

"So it would seem." McBride stroked his forehead as if to smooth out the accumulation of creases. "How was the Brigadier?"

"Defending himself, mainly."

"Against Norris?"

Lancaster nodded. "Incidentally, Norris told me the P-Five is under consideration for Roman Candle. Is that correct?"

"The P-Five?"

"Yes."

"Where did he get that idea?"

"From one of last week's Round Robins apparently."

"Well, he's mistaken. Quite mistaken."

"I thought he must be. I can't remember having seen anything to that effect."

"Are you sure you didn't misunderstand him?"

"He mentioned it twice."

McBride pushed some papers about on his desk and said: "Well, I suppose we're all entitled to an occasional aberration. There's enough on our plates to surprise me it doesn't happen more often. . . . Thank you, David." And that was that.

Around eleven he came into Lancaster's room, something he rarely did at any time. He had the Round Robin reference clip with him. "It's as I thought, David. I got these from the strongroom just to make certan. There's nothing here about the P-Five and Candle—absolutely nothing. I think we should contact Norris and put him on the right lines. Will you do that for me?" Dryly, he added: "We don't want the Minister more confused than he already is."

Lancaster rang Norris on the scrambler. "I know," Norris said at once. "I've been talking out of the back of my head. I was going to call you myself about it. No harm done, I hope. I can only think yesterday morning's shunting exhibition didn't do me any good; either that, or I'm in need of a long holiday. . . . Sorry, Lancaster."

Sloan's office had an untidy, impermanent look, as if he had only recently taken possession or was shortly about to depart. When Lancaster brought the suitcase he hadn't gone beyond the outer room, but this time Sloan's assistant ushered him through. There were sandwiches and a glass of milk on the cluttered desk.

Rising, Sloan said: "Ah, Mr. Lancaster."

"Good afternoon. How's the cold?"

"Better, thanks." He started removing some papers from a chair, clearing his throat as if from habit. "Much better. Please excuse the chaos. The painters are descending on us tomorrow so we're preparing to shift farther along the corridor. Couldn't happen at a worse time, but there's no peace for the wicked, is there?" It had the worn ring of an internal joke. "The files are all ready, you'll be glad to hear."

"Did you find them useful?"

"Oh yes."

Lancaster almost said: "In what way?" But he was there as a go-between, not as a partner, and he left the question unasked. Instead, continuing to stand, he said: "There's something I feel I ought to let you know."

The close-set eyes fixed on him attentively.

"It's a domestic thing, really. Personal . . . But I thought it wisest to get it out of the way."

"What is it, Mr. Lancaster?"

Lancaster had never imagined he would find it so difficult. "I'm having an affair with one of the department's secretaries." He moved his hands, aware of the wooden quality of his voice. "We've managed to keep it quiet until now. There's been a particular reason for our wanting to do this—"

"May I ask who the lady is?"

"Miss Tierney."

"Mr. Conway's secretary?"

"That's correct." Lancaster moistened his lips. "As I was saying, we've had a particular reason for being as discreet as possible. It so happens that Conway and I don't hit it off. In fact, that's an understatement." (Hadn't he earlier said to Sloan: "We're a team at Weapons Coordination; a bloody good one"? As he spoke he remembered.) "So in the circumstances Miss Tierney and I have done all we could to ensure there's no come-back, no unnecessary difficulties." He paused awkwardly. "D'you see what I mean?"

"Perfectly," Sloan said. "But there's really no necessity for you to have mentioned this." He produced the curious brand of smile that was very much his own: in other men lay most of every man's secrets. "I'm not a priest, Mr. Lancaster." He made it sound like an expression of condolence.

"I preferred to tell you. And if possible I'd like the information to remain confidential."

"As far as I'm concerned I'm sure you'll find it will."

"Thank you."

Easing their way out of the ensuing silence, Sloan said: "Miss Tierney has a flat in Holland Park, hasn't she?"

"That's right."

He'd put her file to good use. "And joined the department in March of this year?"

"About then, yes." Lancaster hesitated, not certain whether to say more. But enough was enough. "Well, I won't delay you. Now I've got to smuggle my suitcase back into the office while the coast is clear." To this extent they were in league.

Sloan opened a metal cupboard. His movements were surprisingly athletic. "I can assure you we're a sight more professional than this rather clumsy business might have led you to believe."

Lancaster took the case. "You'll be in touch, I suppose?"

"If the need arises." Sloan showed his false teeth again. "Good-bye then, Mr. Lancaster. No, no, the other door. That's it."

His gray-suited assistant in the outer office nodded as Lancaster moved through. The long corridor with the numbered rooms was monastically quiet. A priest? Grimly, Lancaster pressed his lips together. He knew this corridor: Walker had been brought here. Sloan a priest? Hardly. A rat-catcher. But how able? How ingenious? Above all, how *quick*? With a person like Sloan it was difficult to be sure, but all the signs were that he was still immersed in groundwork.

# Chapter 6 ] ❦

IN the starlit darkness of the cottage Catherine whispered, "David . . . David," murmuring it like a sigh as she finally curled away from him.

When Lancaster slept he went into oblivion; nothing intruded. He was the first to wake, surfacing to the shadowless predawn light and the silence outside and the soft purr of her breathing. He got up and pulled the curtains aside, staring out at the still lake and the hills beyond. There was a mist on the water, clouds low over the hills. And the floor was cold, too cold for him to become self-absorbed. He padded to the bed and eased himself under the coverings, not disturbing her, leaning on an elbow and watching the dawn swell, watching the colors coming back into her hair and skin. She twitched occasionally, as if frightened by some make-believe or other, but he let her sleep on. "Where were you last night?" he'd asked at the office on Thursday. "I called you twice. . . . An aunt? I didn't know you had an aunt." It was daunting how suddenly jealousy planted itself; as daunting as it was novel to lie with a girl and demand nothing. So much was new to him. Yet only a week ago, in that self-same room, he'd teased her, saying: "You'll never grow up if you believe in love."

She stirred at last and he went on watching her, fascinated. "What's the time?"

"You always ask that. Time's any old thing you want to make it here."

"Give me a clue."

"It's Saturday." He kissed her gently. "Saturday. And tomorrow's Sunday. And we're ten million miles away again."

"That's nice to know."

She moved her hand and desire returned. And for a while then there was no before or after.

Catherine pushed her compact and lipstick into his shirt pocket and they drove into Kilvarna in the Volvo. The weekend would look after itself; only tourists planned their days. As they neared the Lakeside Hotel Catherine said: "Pull in, will you?"

He slowed. "Must we?"

"I'm out of cigarettes."

"You can get them in the village." Fletcher's Land Rover was parked against the gray roadside wall; Lancaster jerked his head. "Odd man out."

"Does it matter?"

"He gives me the creeps."

She seemed surprised. "As bad as that?"

"I can think of better ways of starting a weekend."

"All right," she said easily. "If that's the way you feel. But you can hardly avoid bumping into him altogether."

"Once will be enough. He's a bore, a dreary blunderbuss of a bore."

He shifted gear and cruised toward the village. At the first tobacconist's he stopped. The shop sold bacon and children's clothes as well; Ireland would never cease to surprise him. He thought Catherine had done with Fletcher, but as he settled behind the wheel with her pack of twenty she asked: "Did you bring him any books?"

"No, I didn't." He laughed shortly. "And his libido will have to lump it." His watch showed eleven o'clock. "Where would you like to go?"

"I don't mind."

"South? North? East? West? It's all yours. You say."

"South."

South meant Clare, a world within a world, wild and beautiful, even more remote from twentieth-century squalor.

There was a time when Lancaster couldn't have even partially battened London down—not with the situation as it was. He'd come to Kilvarna during the Walker affair, though only for a matter of hours; it was no place to remain then. He was back at the flat next evening, in touch with Colonel Gray, telephoning Gilligan. There had been a job to do. But that was long before Catherine had set alight this train of self-discovery, exposing secret places in his heart he never knew existed—in his or in anyone's. And now they burned in him. A week, and he was beginning not to recognize himself. For too long he had been accustomed to an unnatural kind of loneliness, the kind that came from the stress of secrecy, discretion bordering on distrust, periodic ruthlessness. It suited some and it had suited him. Once the cap fitted you wore it to the best of your ability, never quite free, never entirely relaxed, never quite what other people were. With Catherine he was safe, but there were secrets even from her, and would continue to be. Was it unrealistic to suppose that once this crisis had passed, once Weapons

Coordination was in the clear, once McBride had finally relinquished that creaking swivel chair of his, there might be a chance to get the hell out of it all? Catherine had set a pendulum swinging.

She sat very straight beside him, lips parted a little, sometimes turning her head when a particular scene caught her eye. He let the roads lead him, now through a deep trench between the breasts of untenanted slopes, now climbing until on every side the green country was spread like a wrinkled map. They lunched outside a small town the name of which he forgot as soon as they left: Banagh, was it? It is impossible to measure happiness, but whether they laughed or were silently contented together they were closer than at any time before.

Catherine said: "You're like a boy today."

"Am I?"

"A boy playing truant."

"Blame yourself for that."

"I'm congratulating myself."

"Smug," he said.

"Unashamedly smug. I've a right to be."

They passed Tulla, reached Sixmilebridge. Voices came to them out of fields and open doorways. Swinging west they threaded their way to Ennis and beyond, going clockwise toward the sea, the country stark and depopulated, the scattered villages at a distance like gray encrustations on the landscape, as quiet and subdued close to as if the plague had struck. Dust and lichen and dead leaves, faces that evidenced the hard life, smears of broom on bare hills, gutters of green along the valleys, sheep and stone walls, bog and scratched soil. And churches like medieval strongholds: God was still needed here.

"It's sad," Catherine said. "Sad but marvelous."

"Not enough wood to hang a man, not enough water to drown a man, not enough earth to bury a man."

"And that's hateful."

"Cromwell coined it."

"Hateful," she repeated forcibly.

"It was a rough world."

"It's no better now."

He lost her for a while in the way that he used to do. Regret, uncertainty, he couldn't put a finger on these sudden retreats. Nor could he joke her out of them; he was learning that he must wait for the mood to pass.

Even so, he said: "You aren't sorry, are you?"

"Sorry?"

"You know what I mean."

She looked at him and he caught a sidelong glimpse of her grave, intelligent eyes. For a fleeting moment she seemed to be reaching for an answer, but then a smile came, and a shake of the head, placating his concern.

Blotches of shadow slid across the hills. Ponies browsed on the chameleon slopes; the cobalt sea glittered in the distance. Spanish Point, Lisconnor Bay—the names were as new to Lancaster as they were to her. Adler didn't belong here, Sloan didn't belong. There would be a time for them again, but not yet, not for a bit. A kind of rashness had entered him. No one had a monopoly when it came to shortlists; his alter ego could weed and ferret too. Only a handful rated as possibles, a round dozen, all with access, all with opportunity. At least half of these could be eliminated out of hand and the remainder provoked instinctive disbelief. Yet Conway had a point, and it was alarmingly logical: the Liaison Section or Weapons Coordination, one or the other. Pank, Tyndall, Dansie, Ridgeway, Lewis, Ruth Smart, Hearne, Margaret . . . Later, he thought dismissively. Not now. Catherine claimed him and Sloan had given them carte blanche.

Waves creamed along the base of the Cliffs of Moher. In late afternoon they came to Lisdoonvarna and Lancaster was back on familiar ground. He went past the pub he knew best; women weren't exactly welcome there. It was strictly a man's place, an unofficial club, a meeting house for serious drinkers and the transaction of private business. But Lisdoonvarna catered for everyone and they stopped for a while at a hotel, as much to stretch their legs as anything, choosing a carpeted alcove in the cocktail bar where there was table service.

"You've had a real Cook's tour of a day."

"I've loved it," Catherine smiled. "Every minute."

"Anywhere special you'd like to dine?"

She put on a spurious brogue. "You must be after forgetting I'm a stranger here."

"You'll never sell me that one. Rafferty's can be fun. What d'you say? It's near Kilcorgan."

They were there by seven. Rafferty's had once been a mansion and there was still a lawn at the rear where in warm weather you could sit under striped umbrellas overlooking a stream. But the light had gone now and there was a chill in the air; they had their drinks indoors. Both then and in the crowded restaurant afterward, Lancaster had no need for careful glances at their neighbors; Conway had diminished. He held Catherine close when they danced. Later they went down into the cellar where a girl with long hair red enough to have warmed your hands on sang her little songs of treachery and betrayal. A bearded guitarist accompanied her, and as she sang she seemed to take upon herself all the cares of the world and its glittering and deceptive sins. There was candlelight and shadow, the press of people on barrels and benches under the cavelike ceiling, the bass notes of the guitar wandering through the melancholy of the voice and the rhythm of beating hands.

It was midnight before they left. Lancaster drove fast under the half-moon, too fast, exhilarated, one arm around Catherine's shoulders. She appealed to him to cut his speed but he laughed and kept the throttle open. The night rushed past.

"Scared?"

"I don't scare that easily. But one of my ambitions is to live to doddering old age." A dog's eyes gleamed in the headlights; the tires snickered on a corner. "When you were young," Catherine said, "I bet you pulled the wings off flies."

Lancaster laughed again. He started on a verse of one of the girl's songs and Catherine joined him, almost defiantly.

> "Some were waylaid,
> Some were betrayed,
> But what did it prove?
>  I ask you.
> The murders repaid,
> The saddest prayers prayed,
> But where was the love?
>  I ask you . . ."

Kilvarna slowed them. "I love you." He'd never said it before. Except for a solitary drunk who signaled in the hope of a lift, the short main street was empty. And, farther along the road, the Lake Hotel was in darkness. Lancaster ran the Volvo onto the cinders outside the cottage and they went in, his arm around her shoulders again, alone together, alone as they'd been all day, but differently now, about to lose their identities in the passion of a renewed beginning and end.

"I love you," he repeated afterward.

"Thank you, darling."

The "darling" offended him; it was so automatic, so impersonal. "Don't use that word."

"Why not?"

"It's a whore's standby."

Catherine was husky with the onset of sleep. "What d'you know about whores?" she murmured. "Were there whores, David?"

He wanted so much from her. The most he had experienced in the past was a lonely mood of self-laceration and an ulcerous longing to make contact with a woman.

"You're not my whore," he said. "Catherine . . . ? Catherine . . . ?" But he was talking to himself.

There was an envelope lying inside the front door when he went to the kitchen next morning, and even before he picked it up he was aware of its origin. *Hear you're in residence*, he read, *and my spies have never been wrong yet. So how about a civilized jar or two? Rescue me from the savages, in fact.* Fletcher's heavily scrawled initials had pierced the cheap paper.

[ 98 ]

Angrily, Lancaster screwed the note into a ball. It must have been under their feet when they'd returned home. Didn't the man realize when he was *de trop?*

He lit the stove and got the coffee started, then ran a bath and shaved. The weekend had already passed its peak. Now there was the thought of Fletcher to dog the day, the journey to Dublin and the London flight. Time never let up for long: nothing lasted. He took the coffee into the bedroom and woke Catherine, sitting beside her.

"You've got me, you know. I'm hooked."

She kissed him. "No one's told me that so early in the morning."

"So I should hope."

Whatever he had previously hungered after had never been enough. More could be shared than he had believed. There was an ache in him, an ache and a glow, everything he felt inextricably woven together. All at once, it seemed, she had become indispensable to him.

He stretched out beside her, content with that, not too serious, not too flippant, anxious to admit that his life had entered a new dimension, that the future was no longer empty of promise, that qualities one admires are not always beyond one's reach. Solemnly, amusedly, Catherine listened, answering his questions, asking her own. Even the silences were eloquent. For much of the time there was nothing else in the world except themselves and the bed and the four walls and the advancing morning set like a blue tile in the window. Yet Lancaster couldn't keep London entirely at bay; on and off vivid little cameos intruded, part of a malaise that was his and his alone.

"Like the confessional, David . . ." McBride had four walls, too; McBride and others.

They went to the Lake Hotel at noon; nowhere else in the village could they lunch. Inevitably, the Land Rover was in the forecourt. "There's your sore thumb," Catherine said. And Fletcher's voice boomed from the bar into the entrance lobby. "Not only mine," Lancaster retorted. "Still, there's safety in numbers." It wasn't like the previous Sunday; there were several cars, a fair-sized crowd.

Fletcher spotted them almost at once. Swiveling on his stool he called above the hubbub: "David! Why've you been avoiding me? And you, young lady?"

"We were down in Clare."

"What's wrong with Galway? What's wrong with Kilvarna?"

"Nothing."

"Well, you can't dodge me forever." The deep voice, the grinning, red-flecked eyes. "Those born to be shot never get hanged. What are you drinking?"

The men nearest Fletcher moved away, as if grateful to be released. "Morning, Mr. Lancaster," the barman nodded. "Welcome back, miss."

"Thank you. And hallo."

" 'Back'?" Fletcher said. "What d'you mean, 'back'? She's one of us. Only difference is she doesn't live just round the corner. . . . Cheers, anyway. Good luck. Great to see you."

Fletcher somehow had the power to make Lancaster feel that a week hadn't elapsed since they were last together. It was always like this; a week, a month, a whole winter—how long didn't matter. Fletcher seemed to blot out the passage of time, swamping everyone with his bulk, his voice, his demanding sameness. Suffering his company, Lancaster invariably feared the possibility of a sudden outburst, violence, some madness of the tongue. Up at the farm he had once seen Fletcher strike a man: once was enough, and Fletcher had been sober then.

"How's London, young lady? How's the swinging city?"

Catherine tilted her head. "So-so."

"What d'you do there? You've never told me. Or aren't you a working girl?"

"I'm a civil servant."

"Rubbish."

"Ask David."

"Why should I bother with him while you're about? A civil servant?"

"Yes."

"Christ," Fletcher said and stared at her, his thoughts showing. "You're pulling my leg. Come on, aren't you now?"

"I don't pull people's legs."

"Never? You disappoint me."

Lancaster had never loathed him before. Endured him, avoided him, been bored or exasperated; but never this. And the reaction came without warning, resentment spreading as he watched Fletcher's red-eyed mind at work.

He said sharply: "She told you what she does, didn't she?"

"Hallo," Fletcher said with mock surprise. "You still here?"

"You can cut that out as well."

"What's biting you?"

"Cut it out," Lancaster gritted, "d'you hear?"

Fletcher shifted position. "Well, well," he said. "Well,

well." The words came slipshod, tongue-heavy. "Someone's not at his best today."

"I was."

"David," Catherine said. "For heaven's sake."

Lancaster shrugged.

Fletcher gripped him affably on the arm. "Did you lose your shirt at the races or something?"

Lancaster caught Catherine's glance and it was like a warning. With bad grace he said: "Oh, forget it. What are we all having—the same?"

"That," Fletcher said, "is the only question ever worth asking." He was no actor: behind the loose smile and the released pressure of his grip there was a sulking anger. "Whisky, whisky, *saecula saeculorum*."

Catherine steered the conversation in another direction, but it only limped along. After a while she excused herself and left them. When she came back the atmosphere had mellowed a little, though they were still like strangers together, wary, uneasy, even Fletcher. For once he seemed quite ready to turn his attentions elsewhere and they seized the chance. His parting remark to Catherine was: "I'm in the doghouse, young lady. Really in the doghouse. Something's gone wrong with a beautiful friendship."

In the dining room Catherine said: "You don't do things by halves, do you?"

"He was asking for it."

"No more than usual."

"You must be blind if you think that."

"Well, I'm blind then."

"That bloody man . . ." Lancaster didn't finish. He

reached for her hand, pressing it, gaining from the contact. Something moved in the pit of him.

She said: "I do believe you're jealous."

"Is that a crime?"

"You needn't be. And in the circumstances it was hardly flattering."

He looked at her, McBride's other dictum returning like a whisper: "Beware of those who parade their weaknesses, David . . ." He'd controlled his own until now, made do with the short pleasures. Jealous? Yes, he was jealous. And that, as Fletcher had demonstrated, meant vulnerable. So he must watch himself, carte blanche or no. Everything, nothing had changed.

Three hours' drive and an hour in the plane; London was waiting for them under a smudge of fog. But they weren't diverted. A double thud and they were down, then trundling in through the blurred maze of ground lights. A tired customs official marked them clear after hardly a question. The coach filled and pulled away; gradually the city enveloped them. It seemed a long drive to the terminal. As usual they shared a taxi home. A cat fled from the steps of the tall house in Holland Park.

"I hate Sunday nights," Catherine said.

"That's two of us."

"Are you coming in?"

"You're tired. And it's late."

"And you're tired."

"Sort of."

"Tired's another word for selfish. I'm not Miss Tierney until tomorrow."

"You'll be the death of me," he joked and went down the steps to pay the taxi off.

It was two before he reached Bramerton Street. And when he got in he had the curious feeling that the telephone had been ringing in his absence.

# Chapter 7 ] 🐸

"**Y**ES, I did call you, David," the Old Man said. "But not yesterday. On Saturday, it was; around noon. I was hoping to get you to come over to my place for a drink and a chat that evening. I should have asked you on Friday instead of leaving it so late. However, I'll make amends some other time. Sarah, I know, would like to see you again before too long." Something must have showed on Lancaster's face, because he added: "It was nothing to do with what's uppermost in our minds. No . . . actually, my intention was to tell you about it myself."

"Oh?"

"I'm leaving the department, David. I'm pulling out."

"When, sir?"

"At the end of the year."

"I'm sorry," Lancaster said. "Very sorry."

"Well, a time always comes. One can't go on forever and the wisest thing is to cast off while one still retains most of one's faculties." He smiled privately. "Old dogs find it hard to learn new tricks."

"Is this official? I mean, is it to be generally known?"

"I don't see why not. There have been rumors already, I dare say." McBride rose and went to the window, massaging his thin hands, gazing out as if that was where his interest lay. "It's impossible to speak about the future with certainty, but I think you'll find that George will take over when I go. A decision about that doesn't rest with me, of course. But I expect he will. Indeed, I hope he will." A pigeon planed past at eye level and he watched it, fascinated. "They take such risks, have you ever noticed?" Then he turned, the distraction over. "What I've just said about George Conway is entirely confidential."

"Of course."

"How d'you think you'll work with him?"

"Will I be doing that?"

"I imagine so."

"He may have other ideas about a personal assistant."

"I shouldn't think that likely. Perhaps I shouldn't say this, but I'm more than satisfied."

"Thank you."

"Mind you, I'm sure you'll find George a very different kind of taskmaster. He's not one for delegating, and he keeps his ear very close to the ground. But everyone has his own special style. And a younger man should have the reins, particularly in view of our suspect position."

"We'll be clear by the time the year's out . . . one way or the other."

"I hope so." McBride let it go like a sigh. "I very much hope so. A clean bill to finish with is a natural enough wish. But one way or the other, as you put it, clean bill or no, inevitably things will be different here. The security people will never be so easily satisfied again."

Lancaster frowned. "Surely . . . ?"

"Not after this, David." McBride shook his head. "That's

why George Conway will be such a good man from their point of view."

He lapsed into one of his seeming reveries and hummed vaguely. He looked too slight to carry the burdens he did, unwilling to accept even now that the standards he set and expected in others might have been undermined by someone untrammeled by ethics or honor. Dated, not quite in touch, the keen edge blunted.

"Have you heard anything further from Sloan?"

"No, sir."

"No . . . I suppose that's not to be wondered at. He'll go about his business in his own way. He's hardly likely to send us a daily progress bulletin." McBride might have been speaking about a routine audit.

Lancaster paused at the door. Something needed to be said. "I'll be sorry to lose you, sir. Everyone will be."

"You're very kind, David. We've had a worthwhile association, you and I." Now the smile was frank and outgoing. "As far as I'm concerned it couldn't have been better."

Lancaster had more than Conway on his mind, more than Adler, more than Sloan. Norris continued to puzzle him: it was unlike Norris to be inaccurate. He went as far as taking the opportunity of personally rechecking the Round Robin reference clip when he and Dansie were next at the strong-room together. There was nothing on record, and how he could have expected to find anything when McBride already had gone to the trouble of proving Norris wrong he couldn't imagine. Yet this was the way he had always worked, unable to let go until his instinct was satisfied. Instinct was the most reliable guide; instinct was what woke you in the night, the antennae out. "That's sharp of you, Lancaster," Gilligan had once remarked approvingly. "I'd say you'd missed your vocation."

But his main and most urgent preoccupation was nearer home, in Weapons Coordination itself. Every time he passed his colleagues in the corridor, entered their offices, spoke to them on the telephone, read their circulated memoranda, he appraised them in the light of what only he and McBride and Conway knew. Deliberately so now, with intent. Time was passing and there was no telling how profitable Sloan's field inquiries would be, or how prolonged. But one thing was clear. There were more obvious discards than Sloan, with his methodical approach, might have been prepared to accept at so early a stage. The Old Man was out, Conway was out, Catherine was out. Margaret, his own secretary, was almost certainly out. Dansie, too. Pank and Tyndall, ditto. . . . Instinct again; instinct made any short-list shorter. Only five or six at most were even remotely possible suspects, and even then Lancaster had to stretch his imagination to the full. Over and over he kept reminding himself that the department was hand-picked, periodically vetted, subject to spot checks. Against which he weighed the classic pressures brought to bear from the outside; the personal vanities, grudges, quirks of personality that could draw an individual voluntarily into the spy webs. He didn't need to have been acquainted with Walker or have to remember those death-in-the-heat handshakes to understand what it took.

There had been nothing in the papers about Adler's defection. The Monday lunchtime editions were front-paged with a West End fire and the story of a British mer-

chant seaman, appeal for clemency in respect of his conviction for a multiple murder in Bordeaux during the summer.
Albert Chance; the irony of the name registered more than
anything. But no mention of Adler, then or at any time.

For ten days Adler had been a private ghost, rarely spoken
of by either Conway or McBride, yet always in the background, responsible for Sloan and a score of doubts, a mounting uneasiness, closing the net on someone, somewhere. Lancaster was used to cat-and-mouse, but he couldn't exist with
it forever. The pendulum was still swinging. Because of
Catherine he had grown, acquired an incipient distaste for
himself and his work. Hard? Yes, as hard as she'd said. Of
necessity. But only a part of him; not all, not quite all. There
were other loyalties; the opportunity of something lasting,
honest, devoid of betrayals. He'd betrayed her to Sloan
as it was.

Ridgeway, the most junior of the male clerks, brought
some papers to his desk in midafternoon. "Gather it's official,
Mr. Lancaster."

"What is?"

"About the boss."

"When did you hear?"

"Just now. Miss Smart told me. I suppose it's what we've
all been expecting." He waited, ready to go, ready to stay,
a small man with dark, finger-waved hair and a thin black
boomerang of a moustache. News spread like wind-blown
seed when there were no restrictions on it, passing from room
to room. And this was a headline. "Does that mean Mr. Conway will be taking over?"

"I couldn't say."

"It's the general feeling."

"Oh yes?"

Ridgeway. Five months in the department, married, one child, ex-R.A.F. . . . Beyond what was on the file Ridgeway was a virtual stranger, someone who had distributed champagne around the office after a particularly hefty win on Derby Day and, as everyone knew *ad nauseam*, had been on a seven-port Mediterranean summer cruise. An excess of money or a lack of money; these were among the crude stepping stones that once in a while led somewhere. But this time? Lancaster had summed it up to Sloan: his knowledge of how the staff lived outside office hours was nonexistent— unless they happened to be friends.

Now Ridgeway said: "I suppose we'll be informed pretty soon, won't we?"

"How d'you mean?"

"About Mr. Conway."

Lancaster shrugged. "I really don't know the answer to that."

Ridgeway? Adler was there, always there, like a ghost to be laid. Ridgeway? Lancaster wondered, and watched him go.

He dined with Catherine that evening and they went to a cinema. McBride was referred to only briefly, early on. "You were right," he said and she nodded. "My middle name's 'I-told-you-so.' "

During the interval she rested her head on his shoulder. He couldn't seem to remember a time when he'd existed without her.

"Something's on your mind."

"No," he lied.

"There is."

"Us."

"Something else."

"No."

Conway rang for him on Tuesday, around twelve-thirty.
McBride was lunching with the Minister and had left the
office. Conway wasted no time when Lancaster arrived. As
soon as the door was shut he said: "When was the cutout
device first put forward?" He seemed always to want to rat-
tle you. There were all manner of cutout devices. "You
know"—he flipped finger and thumb—"the one for Candle."

"It never came to anything."

"I'm aware of that. When was it mooted, though?"

"D'you want a guess, or a copy of the Minute?"

"A guess."

"Six weeks ago."

Conway nodded. "And who suggested it?"

"What is this, a quiz?" Lancaster took out a cigarette.
Something was up. Conway wasn't leading him by the nose
for nothing. "McBride."

"The suggestion was Minuted?"

"Naturally."

"And the Minute was marked for internal circulation
only?"

"It should have been."

"Well, it was." Conway pushed the green sheet of foolscap across the neat desk; the punch holes were slightly torn,
as if it had been taken quickly from its file. "D'you remember that meeting?"

Lancaster blew smoke, narrowing his eyes as he studied

the Minute. He remembered, all right. Only four had been present—McBride, Conway and himself, plus Jardine from Experimental Weapons; it wasn't a formal meeting so much as a discussion. Woomera had reported that when the proximity fuse activated Roman Candle's warhead the explosive clusters occasionally failed to separate. It was an immensely technical matter which normally would have been passed back to Guildford. But McBride, with his capacity for springing surprises, suddenly suggested the introduction of a simple electronic cutout to assist in making the scatter instantaneous. Jardine had drawn a rough sketch to allow McBride to show exactly what he meant and had then agreed that, on the face of it, this was probably the answer. In fact he'd gone as far as to say he was "pretty damn sure," and amid laughter McBride had finished: "Laymen sometimes have their uses, Roy—do you admit that now?"

"Yes," Lancaster said. "I remember the meeting very well."

"And you'll remember, about three weeks later, Jardine reported that for various reasons the idea just wasn't on."

"Yes."

"Right." Conway stood up, flicking a speck of ash from his sleeve. "The original suggestion was Minuted here, the Minute didn't circulate beyond this department, and Jardine was the only other person involved. Agreed?"

"Agreed."

"Well, then, it may interest you to know that C.I.A. has informed us Adler's added a postscript or two to what I managed to get out of him the other evening. And one of them concerns the proposed cutout modification—a cutout modification that never was." He let it drop like a stone, then paused. "If that doesn't put the spotlight on this department, tell me what does."

Lancaster stared at the Minute: it was dated August 20th.

"This particular penny-packet was leaked on the strength of an internal Minute, a Minute, incidentally, that died a death on our own files. It was never canceled out, never superseded. Jardine telephoned McBride and that was that. The idea evaporated, as most amateur ideas do." Conway didn't care whose toes he trod on. "But it's given us the best clue to date. If you're about to say 'what about Jardine?' don't bother. You might as well point at the Minister himself. This is where the leak is—here, right here."

Glancing up, Lancaster said: "When did you get this from C.I.A.?"

"An hour ago." There were other papers centered on Conway's desk; he waved a hand over them, but kept them to himself.

"Does McBride know?"

"He does. And I've just finished speaking to Sloan."

"Sloan? *You?*"

"I'd have thought he was the party most vitally interested."

"Of course, but—"

"Someone's pushed his luck once too often, Lancaster. Special Branch has been needing a head of steam, and now Sloan's got one." Conway was straightening his tie, vindicated. "What the hell does it matter who gave it to him so long as he uses it?"

Lancaster bit back a retort. Carefully, he said: "It was common knowledge amongst those concerned here that this cutout suggestion had fallen on its face. If the leak's so persistent why weren't Adler's people fed with that information, too?"

"They may have been. But Adler defected ten days ago, less than a fortnight after Jardine reported back to McBride. He can't be expected to know what was in the pipeline at the time he crossed."

Conway had it all sewn up. What was more, he couldn't be faulted.

Catherine wasn't in the outer office. Lancaster went straight to his own room and sat at his desk, deep in thought. Margaret had already gone to lunch and, before long, Hearne looked in on the way to his.

"Squash tomorrow?"

"Sure."

"Good-oh. Don't work too hard."

Alone again, Lancaster rested his chin in his hands, fingers tapping his lips. August 20th had been a Friday—and on that Friday night Catherine had gone with him to Kilvarna for the first time.

# Chapter 8 ] ✦

**H**EARNE beat him in three straight games: 9-5, 9-5, 9-7. They were more evenly matched than the scores made out, but Lancaster wasn't at his best. He wasn't concentrating. Time and again Hearne kept catching him with a low fast shot down the backhand side and then killing his return with an angled volley that found him vainly at full stretch.

"Five bob you owe me," Hearne panted after the second game. "Double or quits?"

"Why not?"

Lancaster thought he might take him when they were 7-all, but after a seesaw for the serve Hearne broke through and it was all over.

"That makes a change, I must say," Hearne grinned, flopping against the wall.

"Too good, much too good."

"When did it last happen?"

"Three in a row?" Lancaster flipped sweat away. "You were in cracking form."

"Don't know about that, but I've certainly shifted a pound or two." Idly, Hearne slammed the ball down the court. "Thanks, David."

They went up the stone steps to the locker room. After the resonance of the court their voices seemed deadened. No one else was there. They sat limply on the bench seats, towels draped about their shoulders, mopping themselves, heads back as if they were suffocating. Hearne's jacket hung on a peg nearby and he made a long arm to fish out a packet of cigarettes. He was of slighter build than Lancaster, with a high intelligent forehead, well-set eyes and nose and very flat ears. Apart from a slight weakness around the mouth, which spoiled his profile, he would have been more than good-looking. But what he lacked physically was compensated by a slightly rakish air and a throwaway ease of manner that could be devastatingly attractive to women.

"How's your love life, matey?"

Lancaster's expression was indecipherable.

"Crest of the wave or nonexistent?"

"Crest of the wave."

"Linda? Is that the one? I met her once, a very luscious—"

"God, no."

"Hidden from sight, is she?"

"Not exactly."

Hearne blinked through the smoke. "You're a tight old so-and-so. Never give a thing away until it suits, do you? You'll be telling me next you didn't know about the Old Man."

"I didn't."

"Come off it, David."

"He mentioned it on Monday."

"Only then? I thought you two were cheek by jowl. What did he let on about Conway?"

"Nothing."

"D'you expect me to believe that as well?"

"I don't see why not."

Hearne rubbed his scalp. "God help us if Conway gets it, that's all I say. If I know our George he'll have us numbering off from the right first thing every morning. Press-ups too, I wouldn't mind betting."

The locker room remained deserted. Lancaster inhaled thoughtfully, then crushed the cigarette butt underfoot. "Changing the subject for a moment . . ." He paused uncertainly, a look akin to apprehension passing across his face.

"Uh-huh?"

"About the P-Five." He kept his voice right down. "Have you ever heard anything about it being in line for Candle?"

"The P-Five? Never, no. What makes you ask?"

"I just wondered."

Hearne glanced at him curiously. "Don't tell me there's something else I don't know." He got up and started stripping off. "What's happened to the yellows, for instance? The trouble with our setup, David, is that the right hand doesn't know what the left hand's doing half the time. Correction—doesn't *want* it to know. Hell, matey, we didn't exactly arrive with the last fall of rain, you and I." He dragged another towel from his locker and wrapped it around his waist. "I'm going to shower off. Coming?"

"In a minute. . . . How's Nadine?"

Hearne turned between the rows of lockers with a rueful smile. For a second or two he didn't answer. Then he said, "Nadine, matey, is Nadine. *Toujours* Nadine," and padded from view.

Lancaster waited until the door stopped flapping. Hearne had left his locker open and his briefcase showed in the gap. A couple of weeks earlier he had seen Hearne open the zip pocket and, with a laugh, produce a sealed pack of kippers and a copy of *Playboy*: "Sinister, eh? What would a trick cyclist make of that?" Now he reached up and slid the briefcase out himself. The zip ran its full length. *Playboy* was still there and Lancaster flipped the pages through. Twice he stopped; once at a nude, once between advertisements, a kind of disbelief possessing him. Time seemed to run to a stop. Then, like someone found out, he zipped the pocket across and pushed the briefcase hurriedly back into the locker.

The only sound as he subsided onto the bench seat was the hum of the air extractors. There were two photostats in Hearne's case.

For a brief yet interminable period the temptation to return to the locker and extract them was almost overwhelming. Stephen. . . . His thoughts were darting in a dozen directions at once and he felt sick, split between what must inevitably follow and a weakness of nerve. But there could be no going back. It was as if the whole of the past ten days had been moving irrevocably toward a moment like this.

Stephen Hearne had copies of the P-Five test reports in his briefcase. Suddenly there wasn't a short-list any more. Suddenly, from one minute to the next.

He went and stood under the shower alongside Hearne and returned to the locker room with him. Afterward they walked through to the bar and drank a couple of pints of bitter each. How Lancaster hid his feelings he never knew. He was alternating between self-loathing and the demands of a creed that insisted that anyone was expendable. Anyone, friend or no. And there were a hundred questions raging silently in his mind amid the casualness of their conversation, questions he'd already asked himself about others, all of them permutations of the same basic query—why? One knew one's friends best.

Practically the last thing Hearne said to him was: "No wonder I pipped you tonight, David. You're only half fit." They were on their way out. "Look at you."

"Balls," Lancaster said, and wiped his glistening forehead.

They went to the tube together. Hearne bought a newspaper and brandished it in a parting wave. "Night, then. See you tomorrow." A grin, and he was gone, cheerful in his ignorance. For five minutes Lancaster signaled every passing taxi in vain. It was ten past eight before he got one.

"Where to?"

"St. John's Wood."

He gave the address of the Old Man's house and leaned back, feeling empty, frightened. McBride would know what to do.

The house was Victorian, at the end of a cul-de-sac. Lights showed through the colored glass in the front door and in the curtained rooms to either side. Lancaster pressed the bell and waited. It had begun to spit with rain, but he hardly noticed. For an hour now nothing had seemed quite real, and being here was no exception. Muffled laughter reached him from the room on the right—the dining room; he knew it from other times.

No one came, so he rang again. At last a shadow moved

behind the glass of the front door, blurred and wavered and finally solidified into the shape of a woman. The porch light clicked on and the door opened almost simultaneously.

"Yes?" It was Sarah McBride. Her eyes widened in surprise when she saw Lancaster. "David!" Her voice was as soft as the Old Man's.

"Good evening, Mrs. McBride."

"Come in, come in. You'll get wet if you don't come in."

He stepped into the wide, arched hall with its faded water colors and awful chandelier. She closed the front door behind him and only then did it dawn on him that she was a trifle flustered, perhaps by the possibility of McBride's having totally forgotten he'd invited him. Something of the sort had once happened to Conway.

"We've . . . we've a few friends—" she began.

"I wondered if I could possibly have a word with your husband?"

"Of course. I'm afraid he's at dinner. We've only just gone in . . ." She broke off, fingering her necklace. A staccato murmuring came from the dining room. "Is it to do with the office?"

"Yes," he said. His pulse was thudding as if he'd run.

"I'll tell Andrew you're here." She showed him into the sitting room. Chintz and dark woods. "Do you mind waiting for a moment?"

"I'm very sorry about this, Mrs. McBride."

"Don't apologize. It will be something important. It must be."

She smiled uncertainly and disappeared into the hall: rumor had it that she didn't know what the Old Man did. As if from a long way away Lancaster heard McBride say:

"Sarah? Who, Sarah?" Then: "David Lancaster?" A chair was pushed back. "Please excuse me, everyone. . . ."

Lancaster dug his nails into his palms. Now it was coming. Another betrayal.

When McBride entered he actually looked surprised, as if he hadn't really expected to find Lancaster there after all. "David?"

"I'm here at a bad time. I'm sorry."

"Don't worry about that. What's happened?" He pushed the door to behind him. "Sloan?" he ventured cautiously.

"No." Lancaster's mouth seemed as dry as a kiln. "No, not exactly." Grim and set-faced, he had rehearsed his opening several times, but suddenly he couldn't get any further.

"Sit down." McBride gestured without drama. His eyes hadn't left Lancaster for a moment. "Why don't you sit down?" There were sherry glasses on the side tables; cigarette butts in the ashtrays. The air whiffed of stale smoke.

"I've been playing squash with Stephen Hearne."

"Yes?"

It came with a rush, and when it came it was devastatingly brief. As long as he lived Lancaster was to remember McBride's face and the grandfather clock in the corner measuring out the silence that followed.

"Hearne?" the Old Man said eventually, as if it were a name offered him from the distant past. "Stephen Hearne?"

"Yes."

"In his briefcase?"

"Yes."

McBride seemed to be struck dumb again for a while. Once or twice he made a meaningless little play with his hands. But finally he managed: "Hearne. . . . It doesn't make sense." Where he was in his mind then it was impossible to tell. Lancaster had never seen him visibly shaken before. He picked up a spill from beside the sunken fire and broke it aimlessly. "These photostats—"

"They aren't ours."

"Not ours?"

"They weren't made in the office."

This was brushed aside. "Whatever persuaded you to examine the contents of his case?"

Lancaster shook his head: the Old Man had got it wrong. "Nothing was further from my mind. I merely started glancing through a magazine which was in the zip pocket."

"How did you know it was there?"

"*Playboy*? I didn't. But as often as not Stephen carries a copy. The zip wasn't locked and the pocket bulged a bit, so I just . . ." He ended with a shrug. And he could tell that, despite everything, McBride disapproved.

"Was the case itself locked?"

"I don't know. I didn't check." His answers seemed to be coming very fast. "I was too confused. I shoved the case back into the locker and went straight to the shower room."

McBride snapped the pieces of spill yet again. "Peterson's report, you said, and Norris's Round Robin? Is that right?"

"Yes."

"What time was this, David? Rather, how long ago is it since you parted company?"

"Half an hour."

"And was Hearne going home?"

"I can't say. I assumed so."

McBride walked abruptly out of the room, leaving the door ajar. Seconds later Lancaster heard him saying: "You must forgive me. I'm most awfully sorry, but, er, something's cropped up that's going to keep me for quite a while. I'm afraid you'll have to continue without me. Sorry, so sorry. . . ." Then he came back, shuffling his feet a little as if he were in slippers. Again he shut the door. "This is awful, David . . . awful." At last it seemed to have sunk in. "Where does Hearne live?"

"In Wimbledon."

"D'you know the address?"

Lancaster gave it to him. His hands and face were clammy.

"He's married, isn't he? A Belgian girl?"

"Yes."

McBride went to the bookcase in the alcove beside the fireplace. A telephone was there and he lifted the receiver, screwing his face in an apparent effort to remember the number he wanted. Then he dialed and the dull sound of the ringing tone punctuated the heavy ticking of the clock. Nervously, Lancaster lit a cigarette, trying not to allow his thoughts to focus on Hearne.

"McBride here, sir. Yes . . ." Lancaster guessed he was on to the Minister. "There's been a lead. One of our people. I can't say more, but I'll call on you personally later if I may, later tonight. . . . No, it's only come to a head during the last hour or so, more by chance than anything. . . . Quite blatantly, it seems, with a minimum of concealment. . . . With your permission I propose calling our mutual friends immediately and getting an investigation started. . . . Oh yes; yes, that's understood." He listened for several seconds, nodding. "Thank you. . . . I'll see to that, yes. And I'll be around later, as soon as I can. . . ."

McBride dabbed the rest down, paused, then dialed a second time. "What was the address again?"

Lancaster repeated it.

"Who is that?" McBride asked into the phone. Under the lamplight his skin was gray. Whoever he spoke to wasn't Sloan; the voice was altogether different. And he didn't introduce himself. "The Minister knows about it," he finished. "Hearne, yes; Stephen Hearne," and listened to the address being confirmed. Then, after saying that he was to be called back as soon as possible, he hung up. He was very skilled, very practiced, and hadn't said a word too many. But he looked drawn as he turned toward Lancaster. "There aren't any children, are there?"

"No, sir."

"I'd like you to stay until they telephone, David." McBride sat down, what seemed like pity lingering in the strained eyes. "It's come to this, then," he said, with an air of defeat. His knuckles would be rapped now: the government always needed a scapegoat. "Unbelievable . . . unbelievable." Then he looked steadily at Lancaster. "He's a friend of yours, isn't he? A personal friend?"

"Yes."

"What could have got into him?"

"I don't know."

"Are there money troubles? Husband-and-wife troubles?"

"I really couldn't say."

"You mustn't hold back out of loyalty, David."

"I'd really rather not answer anything along those lines."

The Old Man massaged his hands as if studying the bone structure. "I can understand how you must be feeling, but these are the questions that spring inevitably to mind."

Lancaster said, "Two photostats prove nothing, surely? I'll be honest with you"—he hesitated—"I nearly didn't report this. I . . . I felt sure Stephen must have an explanation. And, for all we can tell, he may have."

Their eyes met. "In the present circumstances," McBride said quietly, "any explanation will need to be exceptional. To begin with he has broken the department's first commandment, and no one does that by accident—particularly if, as you say, these photocopies weren't made in the office."

"Perhaps, but—"

"How will he explain that, d'you imagine?"

"I wouldn't know."

"Does he live well?" McBride slipped it in.

"Not in the lap of poverty."

"Above his means? Does his wife have money? You've been to his home, I take it."

"Yes, I've been to his home," Lancaster said, but went no further. Stephen would be at the house by now. Did he live above his means? Yes, on his own admission. Did Nadine have money? Not that Lancaster knew of. But he wasn't going to volunteer it; this was for others to discover, this and more.

Gazing at the carpet as if mesmerized by the pattern, McBride muttered: "What I find so incredible—all else apart— is that Hearne shouldn't so much as put a lock on what you tell me he was carrying. That's sailing near the wind, if you like."

"It's his way."

"How d'you mean?"

"He's casual. Off-hand."

"So, I believe, was Vassall. But Vassall could be neat and tidy when it mattered."

"Don't you think—with respect—a comparison like that is jumping the gun a bit, sir? After all—"

"I know, I know." McBride made a mollifying gesture. "But as far as Hearne's work in the office is concerned, and that's what I'm going by, I've always found him particularly methodical and discreet. Observant, too."

"He spotted the cutdown on the yellows, I must say that."

"Did he now?"

"Yes."

"He remarked on it?"

"Oh yes, more than once."

McBride glanced at his watch, reminded himself. "I must telephone Conway. . . . But perhaps I'd better wait until that call comes." Close to he looked dreadfully tired; and he'd taken to humming again, filling gaps with it. "George told you, didn't he, about the postscript from Adler and where the finger pointed?"

Lancaster nodded. "Yesterday."

"One of George's great qualities is that he's objective, totally objective. Where the leak was didn't matter as far as he was concerned so long as it was plugged. . . . By contrast, I've hoped against hope that my department would be cleared. It makes it so much harder when you know a person. . . . You must feel that, David. You must be feeling it especially in view of the way this has come about." A searching glance as he touched Lancaster sympathetically on the shoulder. "Would you care for a drink? A whisky, perhaps?"

"Thank you."

"If I need one I'm sure you do."

He went to the sideboard and poured two small measures. Lancaster swallowed his neat. A muscle to one side of his mouth kept twitching. They'd be well on the way to Wimbledon. Sloan, he supposed. Sloan had something to get his ferret teeth into at last. "Mr. Hearne? I wonder if I could have a word with you for a moment? Alone, please. . . . Detective Superintendent Sloan, Special Branch." It wasn't hard to picture the scene.

As if he were reading his thoughts, the Old Man said: "He'll deny it, of course. He'll deny everything. They always do." He seemed to have made up his mind about Hearne already.

Sarah McBride tapped on the door and put her head round it to say: "We'll be taking our coffee in the dining room, Andrew."

"Do renew my apologies."

"They quite understand. When do you think you'll be finished? I'd like everyone to be able to come in here before too long."

"Soon now. But then, my dear, I'm very much afraid that I shall have to go out. I'll try to spend a little while with them, but it couldn't be for many minutes."

"Oh," she said, then mustered a smile. "Ah well, I suppose it can't be helped."

It was exactly nine-thirty when the telephone rang, and though they were waiting for it Lancaster started. "Yes?" McBride said. Then, for what seemed a long time, he listened, fingers tugging at the other ear. "I see," he said finally. "Well, you know best. You must take whatever steps are necessary. I have to see the Minister, which I'll do later tonight, but one thing I can say now. No publicity, is that

clear? On no account let the press get wind of this. . . .
Very well. Good night."

Lancaster had got to his feet.

"He's being questioned," McBride said. "One can't go
into details on an open line, but I gather nothing else was in
the briefcase—nothing else incriminating, that is."

The Old Man was on the point of telephoning Conway
when Lancaster left. The rain had stopped but the streets
looked lacquered under the lights. He walked to the nearest
bus stop, boarded the first bus to come, got off when it
turned into Oxford Street and found a taxi to take him home.
He'd mastered emotion until now, let his nerves work for
him. But there was no longer any need and he fell onto the
bed as soon as he reached the flat, trembling uncontrollably,
reaction setting in. Within the last twenty-four hours he had
come down to a personal short-list of three: Ruth Smart,
Ridgeway and Stephen Hearne. Ridgeway he'd discarded
first, then Ruth. He would have been on desperately thin
ice with either, and the necessary degree of social contact
was lacking. Not so with Stephen. The ice was scarcely less
thin, yet with him there was opportunity; with him there
was knowledge of an uneasy marriage, restlessness, an over-
draft. It wasn't much to go on, but it was better than nothing.
Conway's latest disclosure had demanded action; Weapons
Coordination was well and truly in the net.

Lancaster stared blankly at the ceiling, never so frightened, never so alone. It was done now; done in panic, done
crudely, but done. He must work on it, build on it, shut his
mind to Stephen and Nadine as he once had shut his mind
to Walker.

He remained on the bed for at least an hour. When he eventually got up he went straight to the desk and typed an unsigned letter to Fletcher. He was keeping away, it said. He didn't know when he'd be over again. The situation was critical and he wouldn't be in touch for a while, not even by letter. So don't expect anything. And for Christ's sake don't prod. Lay off and wait. *Wait* . . .

The envelope he addressed to Martin Brain c/o Tythe Barn Inn, Lisdoonvarna, where Fletcher made a weekly collection of mail. Then he went out and posted it at the far end of the King's Road, as sure as he could be that he hadn't been tailed, but dogged as before by the insistent, day's-long drumbeat of fear.

Part Two ] ❧

# Chapter 9 ] 🐾

THE telephone woke him. He jerked into a sitting position, gathering his wits. Alarm was never far away. Five past six. . . . He fumbled for the light switch.

"Yes?" he asked thickly.

"McBride here, David. Sorry to disturb you so early, but there are two things."

"Yes, sir?"

"First, as far as the office is concerned Hearne is indisposed. Is that clear?"

"Yes."

"Second, don't bother to put in an appearance this morning. I'd rather you went around to see his wife."

"I was thinking of doing that."

"You were? It's the very least we can do, I feel, and you're the closest to her of any of us." The Old Man sounded like death. "I hear she's in not too good a state. Hearne's no longer at the house, d'you see? Find out if she's in any immediate need, that kind of thing."

"Very well, sir."

He hung up. It was still dark outside, dark and silent. He swung his legs off the bed and lit a cigarette, thinking back, thinking forward. Tuesday had been the crucial day; that evening he had gambled by smuggling out a mixed bag of yellows and Round Robins, taken them to Waterloo and copied them on one of the Docustat machines. Waterloo was the station Hearne used. Wiped clean, fingerprints removed, he had handled the copies with a towel when sliding them into *Playboy*, working quickly, listening like a thief, in the grip of a devil of obedience.

McBride was right; Hearne would deny everything—inevitably. Yet how would he account for the other things, still to be done? Given time and the right conditions you could fabricate a case against anybody; Walker was proof. But with Hearne there hadn't been time. This was the best Lancaster could devise, Hearne the most promising victim, the only one who gave him any sort of chance.

Hard? So what? But never again. Never, never again. Already he'd been driven to his very limits. If he got away with this it would be for the last time. Fletcher could go hang, Fletcher and the others along the line. He wanted Catherine. Life without Catherine was becoming meaningless. Christ, he thought. Oh Christ. . . . And put his head in his hands and rocked back and forth, back and forth.

He arrived in Wimbledon soon after ten. Hearne lived in one of those small modern estates with communal landscaping; he'd moved there a couple of years ago and, with his cultivated gift for self-deprecation, had described the houses as being all made of ticky-tacky and all looking just the same. It was, in fact, an immensely pleasing development in an expensive residential area and Hearne had more than once complained that, financially, he had bitten off more than he could reasonably chew. "But you know Nadine, matey, she wants things now. To blazes with how many cherrystones there are on the side of her plate; she's a this-year girl."

Temple Court: Lancaster turned left and parked the Spitfire under the old cedar. Hearne's Mini-Cooper was standing on the garage run-in outside No. 3. Lancaster would willingly have walked on by; he was dreading this. But the necessity of getting into the house propelled him through the gate and up to the smart pink door. Even if McBride hadn't suggested his calling he would have done so. It was vital that he did, and McBride had a streak of compassion in him which could always be played upon if an explanation had been necessary. McBride was as good as an ally any day. But say Nadine wouldn't let him in? Suddenly the familiar tentacles of alarm were squeezing his heart.

He wasn't kept in suspense for long. The door opened after only a few seconds and a tall man with pitted cheeks and horn-rimmed spectacles gazed out at him impassively. Sloan had got his search warrant, then.

"Yes?"

"I'd like a word with Mrs. Hearne, please."

"Mrs. Hearne isn't here."

As evenly as he could, Lancaster said: "I'm from Weapons Coordination. Is Superintendent Sloan inside?"

The man's slight hesitation was encouraging, even though he shook his head.

"Look, I'm a colleague of Mr. Hearne's and the Director of Weapons Coordination has sent me down to see Mrs. Hearne. My name's Lancaster. Perhaps you'd be good

enough to tell Mrs. Hearne I'm here." He'd bluffed so often.
"If we're going to argue about this I'd rather do it with the
door closed behind me."

"Just a minute." The man disappeared, but was soon back,
this time with a grim little suggestion of welcome. "All right,
Mr. Lancaster, come in. You'll find Mrs. Hearne in the sitting
room."

A small relief in wood of the Virgin and Child hung on
the wall above the canisterlike umbrella stand; Lancaster
had forgotten Nadine was a Catholic. The man preceded him
along the hall and went up the stairs, leaving Lancaster
alone.

"David?"

"Nadine."

She was by the picture window overlooking the house's
private garden. Lancaster crossed to her quickly and clasped
both her hands.

"Thank God you have come." Her face was white with
strain and the shock of dispossession. "What is this all about?
They have taken Stephen away—"

"I know."

"—for questioning."

"I know."

"Some papers in his case . . . all nonsense. It is fantas-
tic."

Her voice had always had this curiously attractive lilt but
now it was husky, touched with hysteria. She'd been crying;
her eyes were red and they looked enormous in the small,
pale, chocolate-box face.

"When did Stephen go?"

"Last night." She always made great use of her hands. "About midnight. And then, two hours ago, these men came." This with a jerked glance at the ceiling. "Three of them. Detectives. Now they are searching the house from top to bottom. Searching, if you please. For what? For what, I ask you? Stephen is not a criminal." Tears welled up. She sat down, her shoulders shaking. "I am not allowed to speak to him. Also I have wanted to talk to Mr. McBride, but these men ask me not to use the telephone."

"I don't think they can prevent you."

"Well, they do. They say it is better I do not. Better for Stephen."

"McBride asked me to come."

"What is happening, then? What is this all about?"

"I can't answer that."

"Can't or won't?"

"Can't," he lied. "But I'm here to help. If there's anything I can do, anything you—"

She wasn't listening. "You were with Stephen last night, weren't you?"

"Yes."

"Well, he was hardly home and this man came—no, two men. Sloan, or something, and another. They talked with Stephen, in private, without me." Her eyes blazed suddenly; anger was there. "And then, very late, he asked me to pack a nightcase for him as he was going with this . . . this Sloan."

"What did he tell you?"

"That it must be some kind of crazy joke. . . . Which it is, it must be. . . . I thought he would soon return and I

[ 137 ]

waited. Waited and waited. Then, this morning . . ." She looked at Lancaster helplessly. "What is Stephen supposed to have done that is so terrible?"

"Take it easy, Nadine."

"How can I?"

"If Stephen says it's a joke, then that's what it is. He'll sort it out. There must be an explanation."

"An explanation for what?"

"Whatever it is. The papers he had, I suppose."

"You don't know?"

"I told you." He offered her a cigarette and she took one; it quivered between her fingers. "I'm as much in the dark as you are. McBride rang me to say that Stephen had some trouble and would I make a point of coming. . . . I'm here to help," he repeated. "What can I do?"

"Get Stephen back."

"I can't promise that."

"I don't know where he is and I am asked not to leave the house." Her eyes flashed again. "I would not, anyhow, not with these men here. They are going from room to room. And they tell me nothing. It is monstrous. I am as good as under arrest myself."

She stubbed out the cigarette after only a few agitated draws. A thump sounded from upstairs, as if something heavy had been shifted.

"Speak to Mr. McBride for me, David. Ask him to telephone."

"Of course."

She sobbed silently. "I have a right to know what Stephen is supposed to have done."

"How are you off for money? To tide you over. You've only to say, Nadine."

Gradually Lancaster quieted her. She had badly needed someone there, someone on whom to shed her pent-up distress. Talking was better than not talking; tears with a friend were better than tears alone. He would have stayed as long as was necessary, waiting his chance. In the event it came quite soon. As if with an effort she brushed a strand of blond hair from her face and, with a kind of desperation, said: "Would you like coffee?"

"Only if you're having some."

As soon as she left the room he moved; there was no hesitation. His gaze had already been roving, apparently embarrassed. An envelope containing twenty-five pounds in used notes was slipped under the green wall-to-wall carpet at a point where the tacking was loose and lifted easily. Another, with a photocopied Woomera report on Roman Candle's latest test launching went into Volume IX of *Everyman's Encyclopaedia* on the open bookshelves; another, with copied Guildford blueprints of the Mark 4 nose cone, went between the penultimate pages of an old but apparently little-used edition of Newman's *Apologia Pro Vita Sua*. The envelopes were all from Hearne's desk at the office and Lancaster touched them only with his display handkerchief; the books, too. A minute, barely more, and he had done what he'd come to do. Well before Nadine returned he was at the window, staring out at the chrysanthemums and the neat square of lawn.

"Sugar?"

"Please . . . two."

She left her cup untouched. "This work of Stephen's . . . your work . . . is it so secret?"

"Yes, it's secret."

"He never speaks of it to me." There were fears behind the mask, growing fears. "He never has."

"That's inevitable."

"If I don't really know what he does, how can I know what he might have done?" And then, with tell-tale aggression: "It is not only his work that he does not speak to me about."

"Don't talk like that."

"It is true . . . true. For a year or so now—"

"Come on, Nadine. Thinking this way doesn't help you, and it won't help Stephen. And he's going to need your help."

She stared at him. "You *do* know something, David."

"No."

"It may not be some kind of crazy joke after all; is that what you are saying?"

"How can I answer that?"

They were back where they had begun. Now and again footsteps padded overhead. Lancaster stuck it for an hour before leaving. Yes, he would have a word with McBride. Also, he would discover what he could himself and let her know, as soon as possible. Yes, he promised. For what it was worth he reckoned it would all blow over—though that, he agreed, didn't make her lot at the moment any easier. But it could only be the result of some ghastly misunderstanding. Hell, he knew Stephen as well as he knew anyone, and they didn't come any better. . . .

"Good-bye, Nadine." A taut smile. "Chin up."

She had started to cry again as she closed the door. He

walked to the Spitfire, aware of being watched from one of the first-floor windows, feeling the weight of someone's scrutiny. If Sloan's men had been downstairs he would have used the bathroom, unscrewed the bath panel and planted the envelopes there, or behind the medicine chest, or taped them to the back of the bull-fight print in the loo. But luck had been with him; made it easy.

There was no sense of triumph; he was still on the high wire. If he felt anything at all as he pulled away it was a creeping surge of shame, as if he'd just debased himself with a prostitute.

He drove home, then took a bus to Whitehall. Nothing that could nail him was in the flat, absolutely nothing. The dangers were elsewhere. Ever since Norris had corrected his twice-made comment that the P-Five was being considered for Roman Candle Lancaster had sensed that something might be happening behind his back. He wasn't sure and he could be wrong; the chances were that he was. But it had helped to panic him.

*All passes to be shown.* He fumbled his out and went through, took the lift up to the fifth floor, produced the pass again and turned along the corridor to his own office. It was coming up to Margaret's lunch hour and she was already making preparations.

"Why, hallo," she said, snapping her compact shut and rising. "I'd written you off."

"Well, you can write me back on again."

"There's nothing in your diary. I rang the flat earlier, thinking you were sick or something."

"It was 'or something.'"

[ 141 ]

"Stephen Hearne's sick."

"He was okay last night."

"Exactly. I thought perhaps you'd eaten together and both picked up a bug."

"Not guilty."

"I've flagged the files." Margaret said. "And Ruth left word that McBride wanted to speak with you as soon as you came in. I told her he'd be lucky, but I pinned a note on your blotter just in case.

"Thanks."

He let her go. The desk calendar's Shakespearean quote for the day read: *Things without all remedy should be without regard: what's done is done* . . . and for a few seconds he couldn't bring himself to look elsewhere. Then he followed Margaret from the room and went to see the Old Man, bracing himself. But McBride had gone to lunch, too.

Ruth smiled her exclusive smile and said: "I'll give you a buzz when he's back—all right?"

It was a quarter past two before she let him know. He'd been over to a pub by then for sandwiches and a pint; the food seemed to stick in his throat. Sloan's men would have worked down to the living room by this time, surely? No-stone-unturned Sloan: he was banking on it now.

"How did you find his wife, David?"

"Very distressed, naturally. Bewildered, as much as anything." Lancaster raised his shoulders. "I must say it's a pretty impossible situation for her at the moment, what with Special Branch men going over the place with a fine-tooth comb and preventing her from making outgoing telephone calls. She's as good as imprisoned there, with only the vaguest idea—"

"I don't see how that can be helped. It's in our best interests to soft-pedal everything until we know more. In hers, as well. I spoke with Sloan last night and he's adamant that she is best kept incommunicado temporarily—for her own good, and also for Hearne's. Until Sloan's nearer to the bottom of this only harm would come of her ringing up people indiscriminately. And from our point of view the Minister agrees that we ought to play this as close to the chest as possible."

"Say she needed a doctor? Or a priest?"

"Does she need one?"

"I couldn't say. She's a Catholic," Lancaster finished lamely.

"She's also the wife of a man who, at the very least, has committed a grave breach of security." McBride was as soft-spoken as ever, yet there was a very slight edge. It could have been from lack of sleep; he must have been on his feet most of the night. "No matter how sympathetically—"

"Stephen told her it must be some kind of joke."

"He's sticking to that."

"Oh?"

"Apparently."

In vain Lancaster willed McBride to come out with the news that Sloan had reported further discoveries. A flutter of anxiety moved through him. But his face showed nothing and his voice carried exactly the right amount of vicarious concern.

"She asked particularly for you to contact her."

McBride shook his head.

"It's understandable, sir."

"What did you tell her?"

"There wasn't much I could say."

"Will you be seeing her again?"

"I promised to ring."

"Well, try and make her see that she'll serve herself best by accepting the restraint she's under. Without it she'd be at the center of a scandal by now, and she can't possibly want that. If the worst comes to the worst and Hearne *is* found to have been selling his country down the river, then I'll call on her. But not before."

"And if he isn't?"

McBride looked wearily at Lancaster. "D'you think that likely, David? Do you honestly think that likely now?"

"I don't know what to think. I'm almost as bewildered as Nadine."

"Nadine?" McBride frowned, as if his concentration had been elsewhere. "Who is Nadine?"

"His wife."

"Oh yes, of course."

The Old Man was easy, a pushover. There was nothing to fear from him. He was all but convinced as it was. But Sloan was different. Sloan wouldn't be content with what was in the briefcase; he'd need more than that to combat Hearne's denials, and without something more he might begin to consider an alternative possibility. *The* alternative.

"That's all for the moment, David."

Lancaster nodded and turned away. It was two-thirty. Come on, his mind was urging. Come *on* . . .

He telephoned Nadine from one of the booths in the downstairs lobby. A man answered and pretended he'd got the wrong number, but eventually, after establishing Lan-

caster's identity, agreed to put Nadine on the line. Her ac-
cent seemed more marked than when he had been in the
house, her tone more spirited, and he told himself as he
spoke, "You're a tough little nut," taking refuge in the
thought. There was nothing new to tell, only spurious comfort to offer. Choosing his words carefully, he did his best to
explain that McBride was no better informed than he was.
Whether she believed him or not he couldn't have said, but
she was more subdued by the time she asked: "What made
Sloan come here in the first place? And why last night? Who
told them to descend on Stephen?"

"They keep these things to themselves, Nadine. They
haven't divulged much. But I still say you'll find it has all
been a ridiculous mistake. McBride agrees with me. He's as
shocked as you are, but there's little he can do. It's out of his
hands, d'you see . . . ?" Lancaster paused to clear his
throat. "Have they nearly finished with you there?"

"They are in the kitchen and the garage."

Lancaster's heart sank momentarily.

"In the kitchen and the garage and the sitting room." Her
voice began to break again. "And I shall sue them when this
is finished. When Stephen comes home again I shall get him
to take action. . . ."

"Yes, Nadine."

Still in the sitting room . . . Were they blind? Lancaster
fretted as he left the booth and waited for the lift. Christ,
were they blind?

The afternoon dragged. Lancaster toyed with the accumulation of paperwork heaped on his desk. Catherine came
in once, her smile guarded because Margaret was there, her

request for some information for Conway formal in the extreme. But she revived a longing in him that remained imprisoned at a deep, unlocalized point within. Nothing seemed quite real any more. He had risked so much, survived so much, and this time everything hung by the slenderest of threads, a thread of his own desperate, clumsy making. Catherine and the future; both were dangling. Survival wasn't the only goal. Without Catherine the years ahead would be as meaningless as other men's dreams.

Whenever his phone rang he answered it half in dread, half in anticipation. He couldn't settle, couldn't assimilate what his eyes glossed over. Ridgeway delivered a handful of files; first Tyndall and then Dansie called him up to clarify something relating to a Research and Development Minute. "Sorry to bother you, David," Tyndall began, "but in view of Stephen's absence . . ." The trolley clanked along the corridor and Margaret brought him tea. "Are you all right?" she asked.

"Sure—why?"

"You've got your headachy look. Shall I bring you some aspirin?"

"No," he said. "No thanks. I'm fine." And felt his mouth drag sideways.

It was well after five before Ruth came on to say that McBride wanted him. He went at once, uncertainty like a fist hardening in his belly. Conway was in the room, perched on a corner of the Old Man's desk, and it shook him to find him there.

"Shut the door, David, and come and sit down."

There was silence until Lancaster had settled himself, one of those silences that could have prefaced anything. Conway watched him covertly, a potential enemy always, pretending to examine his manicured nails yet, Lancaster felt, judging him according to some antagonistic instinct. Nervously, he felt for a cigarette.

Then, at last, McBride said: "Sloan has just reported further findings in Hearne's house."

"Oh God." He managed it perfectly, low, like a groan.

"I'm afraid so."

"What, exactly?"

"Copies of a nose cone blueprint and a Woomera launching report—both Roman Candle's."

"And money," Conway put in.

Lancaster felt his mouth drag again as relief swept him. "There's always money in a house." Instinctively he was back on the old defensive tack. Stephen was a friend.

"In an envelope?" Conway clasped his hands around his jutting knee. "Under the carpet?"

"The money is incidental," McBride said. "But these other things . . ." His pained expression was of someone betrayed. "It's tragic . . . frightening."

"And cast-iron," Conway said. He was adopting his bullying tone; facts were facts. "God knows what else will come up, but this alone is enough."

"It's unbelievable," Lancaster said with a shake of the head. "I know him well. I know them both so well."

"Both?" Conway queried, glancing at him.

"Hearne and his wife. Things weren't too good between them, but this . . ." He left it there, a seed-bed for Nadine to develop, a bit of background, then looked across at McBride. "What does Stephen say now?"

But Conway answered him. "I can't see that it much matters what he says." He had no patience with things like that. "What does matter is that they've checked on the documents in his briefcase and they reckon they were made on one of those public photocopying machines you see in department stores and in railway stations. Which means he somehow got the originals out of the office. Which means there's a deal of tightening up to be done in this place."

"The horse has bolted, George," McBride began. "And—"

"That's no excuse," Conway retorted, as if the Old Man were a junior. "In view of Hearne the whole of our internal system needs reexamining. If there's one loophole there are almost certainly others."

"I couldn't agree more, but—"

"The Minister will insist on it. And not only the Minister."

"Yes, George, yes. But here and now I suggest we get our priorities agreed upon. Until Sloan has worked on Hearne and we know more about the extent of the drain of information—"

"Adler's already filled us in on that."

"All right." McBride conceded, restrained by some private discipline. "All right." He was drawn with fatigue and there were dark rings under his eyes. "Nevertheless I put it to you that Hearne is currently Sloan's responsibility and whatever shakeup will follow in the department is not the immediate concern." He put his fingers to his forehead, massaging the creases. "On the other hand there's a rescue operation needed for Roman Candle. And it seems to me that there are two practical things to be done. One is that we have to decide on a cover story to explain Hearne's absence. We can continue with sickness, if you like, or cook up an overseas posting for him, or even—"

Lancaster said: "Whatever we agree on couldn't be effective indefinitely."

"For long enough."

A dribble of sweat moved through his neck hair. "Long enough for what, sir?"

"For some way to be devised of canceling out what has been leaked—as much as possible, anyhow. We've got to put our heads together and see what can be done about feeding incorrect information into the channels Hearne has been using. This sort of thing was done during the war and we can do it now, but only so long as there isn't a song and dance that he's been rumbled."

McBride was really rushing his fences. "Say he won't admit to the existence of any channels?" Lancaster said. "Say he continues to deny everything?"

"Then we'll have to invent channels of our own." The Old Man gazed at Conway as if to silence any objection. "It's been done," he repeated. "And done successfully."

"What about this wife of his?" Conway asked. "Why should she go along with whatever we happen to think is a plausible cover story?"

"We can talk with her."

" 'We'?"

"I will." McBride said. "Not you, David—I'll spare you this time. You've had enough unpleasantness in that direction, more than enough. . . . Yes, I'll do it."

Conway stood up impatiently. "What yarn can you spill her, for God's sake?"

"I don't know about 'yarn.' But I can put it to her that to avoid her being badgered by scandal, we feel it would be as well if she did as we ask. Surely it will be better for her to maintain that her husband has gone overseas, say, than to have to admit the truth to her friends and family?"

Conway shrugged. "We can't put a lid on the truth forever. It will blow up in her face before long. It must, and she'll know it must."

"Perhaps she'll be more prepared by then. She's a Catholic, David tells me. Having a faith to turn to can make things more bearable. At least, that is what one wishes for her."

Lancaster listened, relief taking root. It was beginning to look as though he'd won his reprieve. And time would erase the price of it. It had before and it would again. He couldn't remember Walker in detail, Walker who had protested his innocence also—endlessly, as would Hearne. But to no avail. "He never let on," Gilligan said afterward. "I'll give him that. He never let on who his contacts were."

"We'll talk about this tomorrow," the Old Man was saying. "I think we're all too tired now. I am, for one. . . ."

The past buried itself if you blocked your mind. Everything could be forgotten, everything and everyone—Walker, Stephen, Nadine, Fletcher . . .

"That's all, David."

Lancaster's legs felt weak as he rose and moved to the door. He was as good as in the clear, but he couldn't have stayed much longer without something showing. When he paused to light a cigarette in the corridor his hands were shaking so much that the flame danced like a mad thing.

# Chapter 10 ]

HE lay sprawled on the bed in Catherine's flat with his jacket off and his arms crossed loosely over his face. She was in the bathroom, washing some stockings: "Five minutes, David, that's all. . . . Who'd be a girl?"

He lay as if shielding his eyes from the lamplight and waited for her to finish, his mind churning quietly. After leaving the office he had come straight to the flat. She was like a drug which kept his thoughts from being sucked down where they least wanted to go—back into the dark funnel of feeling hemmed in, of knowing that he was trapped unless he committed himself, of traveling in retrospect through alarm leading to action, the action in turn prickling with uncertainty and then relief. With a drink in hand, watching her prepare supper, and during supper itself, he had been more than usually cheerful. Even though he had lived on his nerves for so long, relief was still the hardest emotion to hide away. "What creamy milk have you been lapping up?" Catherine asked him. "You're purring."

"Any objection?"

"Only if it's not because of me."

Her eyes were empty of all harm or deceit, and he knew

again how secure he was with her. The ice had borne his weight; hour by hour the danger was passing. More than anything he wanted to share this calm of hers, not merely to use it as a temporary haven. Peace and permanence—the longing had begun to possess him. Once the crisis had completely receded, once Fletcher had been dealt with, once McBride's plan of deception—whatever it turned out to be— was launched, he could start to think of the future as a reality. When Conway took over, he would resign; Catherine practically expected it. Anyone could begin again, slough a skin, mold another version of themselves . . . He kept telling himself these things. Even then, with Hearne at bay, with Nadine at her wits' end, a part of him was seduced by the thought that love could become all in life.

"Catherine?"

"Coming."

She sat beside him. He pulled her down and kissed her, lingering anxiety fanning the need to be wanted, made to feel necessary. "Yes?" he asked, brushing her lips with his.

"Yes, what?"

"D'you love me?"

"What do you think?"

"It's never been important before."

In the past he had needed women because he had felt alone without one. They had given him a comfort of sorts, though not all. In any case, resentment was never far away. But Catherine's was not the comfort of a whore; she would untangle him eventually. A time was coming when he would have ceased to be afraid of showing that he was afraid.

She stroked the line of his jawbone, feeling the muscles soften. "When are we going to Kilvarna again?"

"One of these days."

"Soon?"

He said: "I hope so." But he thought: No. Not even soon . . . never.

A reason could always be found: he'd had an offer for the cottage, too tempting to refuse. Kilvarna, he could say, had begun to pall. There were other places, if not in Ireland then somewhere else. From now on, depending on what was said, things would change. He could handle this; lies were his stock in trade. And then he could be done with them as he would be done with Fletcher. He had served Fletcher to the best of his ability and now the break was coming. And Fletcher couldn't stop him. He owed nothing to Fletcher, nothing to anyone. From the beginning he'd been a volunteer, and the *why* to that was buried in his innermost self. Fletcher had become his link one rainy, tree-dripping evening in Green Park when he'd met that sallow-faced man from the embassy and been told with whom to communicate. They'd had their money's worth, over and over; Roman Candle alone had paid for every penny. To his mind, therefore, he had no masters. He had given value, full value, and as a bonus he would counter McBride's intended deception. Then finish.

He stroked her raven-dark hair. "You didn't answer my question."

"Which one was that?"

"Wretch." He'd been good at teasing, but it wasn't so easy to be teased. His fingers tightened on her hair and he pulled gently.

"Ouch."

"That's not an answer."

"Stop it, David . . . Hey! You're hurting."

"Yes?" he asked, laughing, leaning close.

"Yes . . . yes."

"Yes, what?"

"I love you."

"Again."

"I love you."

He released her and she sat up. "You're a brute," she said ruefully. There was no smile. But he laughed again, zigzag veins in his temples. It must be terrible to love and not to be loved in return.

Sloan rang him at Bramerton Street early next morning. Lancaster was in the middle of shaving. His heart missed a beat when he recognized the voice, which was brisk, matter-of-fact.

"I'd appreciate it if you would call at my office before ten. Could you manage that?"

"I think so, yes."

"I won't keep you long, but there are one or two points I'd like to go over."

"Very well. I'll be there within the hour."

"Thank you, Mr. Lancaster."

He wasn't out of the wood yet, but the "I won't keep you" was something to buttress his nerve. He left the house sharp on nine and queued in the King's Road for a bus. By half past he was on his way up the stairs to Sloan's office, and again there was that griping feeling of apprehension, of not being sure. Only fools were overconfident. A phrase was no guarantee. He might be walking into the discreetest of traps. Hearne was probably somewhere in the building and Sloan could have decided on a confrontation. Imagination began to run wild as he neared Sloan's door.

But no. The Superintendent was alone, coat off, tie loosened.

"It's good of you to come so promptly, Mr. Lancaster." He wasted no time. "I wanted to speak to you about the other evening, the one that started this particular ball rolling."

"I'll help all I can." Lancaster sat down. This was where the danger was. With heightened awareness he noticed that the office was as chaotic as before.

"I gather you played squash with Hearne regularly?" Sloan might have been speaking of the dead.

"Once or twice a month, usually."

"And what happened in the locker room was sheer chance, I take it?"

"Absolutely."

"You didn't suspect him?"

"Good lord, no."

"You were just looking for looking's sake."

"I wasn't prying, if that's what you mean. A magazine was protruding from the zip pocket"—was that what he'd said to McBride?—exactly what he'd said?—"and I just pulled it out."

"Hearne having gone to the shower room?"

"Yes. I was finishing a cigarette. I like to cool off a bit first." Lancaster shrugged expressively. "I was dumbfounded, naturally."

"I can imagine."

Sloan's eyes were telling him nothing. With what he thought was guile, Lancaster said: "By elimination, as you know, it was possible to make out a strong case that our department was the source of the leak. But Hearne was almost the last person one could have suspected. Anybody would tell you that. I had possibles, if that's the word, of my own. It's an awful thing to say, I suppose, but in the circumstances—"

"Who were they, Mr. Lancaster?"

"I hardly think it matters now."

"All the same I'm interested."

"Very well, if you insist." Lancaster paused. "Miss Smart, McBride's secretary, and Ridgeway, one of the male clerks."

"You suspected *them?*" Sloan seemed curious.

"Suspected, no, not exactly. But of the dozen people with what you yourself called 'maximum opportunity' they did seem to me . . ." With a show of irritation Lancaster said: "I'd really rather not pursue this. There was nothing to go on. My feelings were purely instinctive, and events have shown how wrong they were."

"Indeed," Sloan said. "Yes, indeed." He crossed his long legs. "Reverting to Hearne—you know he continues to deny all knowledge of what has so far come to light?"

"I heard that, yes."

"It makes things more difficult for us, of course. But denials alone aren't much of a defense."

"Does that mean . . . ?" The question dried on Lancaster's tongue.

"What does what mean?"

"Nothing." He could have kicked himself. "It's hard to think straight knowing Stephen as I do, and having seen what this has done to his wife. . . ."

"I was told you had called on her." Again, Sloan's expression defied interpretation. "We've some way to go yet. There are many inquiries still to be made. I talked with Mrs. Hearne myself last night."

"How was she?"

"Very calm, considering. Inclined, I should have said, to be a shade vindictive."

"Toward her husband?"

"Does that surprise you?"

"Not entirely."

"Has she cause, d'you know? I don't expect I'm telling you anything new when I say that Hearne evidently lived somewhere above his known income."

"It was rather expected of him, I'm afraid."

"I guessed as much." Sloan stroked his nose. "Were there other women?" When he got no answer his mouth curled wryly. "Perhaps that was a little unfair, Mr. Lancaster. But we can find out."

He had a few more questions; not many, not too difficult. Mainly they concerned Hearne's private life and Lancaster stuck to his friendship formula to deal with them. Presently Sloan glanced at his watch and stood up, dragging his coat off the back of the chair. "I'm afraid I have an appointment at ten. My car's outside. Can I give you a lift? Whitehall's longer than you'd think if you're on foot."

He drove the car himself, surprisingly badly. As he straightened into the traffic's flow by the Cenotaph he suddenly asked: "Did you enjoy your trip to Ireland?"

"Ireland?"

"Last weekend."

With an enormous effort Lancaster fought off the weakening rush of panic.

"You and the young lady—the one you mentioned." Sloan was back to his habit of making statements, yet they dangled like baited hooks. "Miss Tierney." He dabbed the brake as a taxi cut in. "You've been under observation, Mr. Lancaster. The entire department has—inevitably. Each and every one of you. Surely that doesn't come as a surprise?"

"I suppose not." Now the urge was to bluster. "I've a cottage over there."

"Oh yes? Well, I envy you." They were past Horse Guards, coming up to Trafalgar Square. Nosing into the curb, Sloan said: "Will this be all right?"

"Thanks."

As Lancaster was getting out Sloan touched his sleeve. "Don't worry; what you told me the other day will remain in confidence. Anyhow, the tailing is off now that we've as good as got our man."

Even with this in his ears it took Lancaster the best part of an hour to decide that, on balance, the interview had gone in his favor. But, God, he'd still got to watch himself.

On one point McBride had already made up his mind— or had it made up for him. Ostensibly, Hearne was to be loaned to the British Military Attaché in Washington; "secondment" he called it. "There'll be no problem; the Minister will arrange for Hearne to be nominally transferred and our people over there will be asked to cooperate. He can be kept on ice this way, at least for a short while."

"He hasn't been charged yet," Conway grumbled. "Then he's got to go before a magistrate. How in the blazes is *that* going to be kept quiet?"

"It was in Blake's case. Blake went in front of the magistrate before normal court business. Nothing was logged in the Register and the press weren't informed."

"That was stretching it."

"A lot of things will have to be stretched from now on, George." The Old Man looked more rested, sounded more in command. "There are ways and means."

"What about his wife?"

"She's going to a hotel down in Hampshire, under another name."

"You've seen her?"

"I had a long session with her this morning. It wasn't easy, but she took my point. In the end she was agreeable."

"You must have the charm of Old Nick, that's all I can say."

McBride didn't much care for that. To Lancaster he said: "She's leaving later this afternoon, David, but don't get in touch with her before she goes. It wouldn't help. I've said my piece and she knows how to contact me."

"Very well, sir."

"I'm sorry"—he made an extenuating gesture—"but it's me she seems to want to rely on at present. She's in a very emotional state. She's Belgian, of course," he added, with untypical naïveté.

"To be honest, I'm rather relieved."

The October sunlight streamed fitfully into the room, making it appear to expand and contract. The three of them formed a triangle, Conway and Lancaster seated at the front corners of the desk, McBride in the creaking swivel chair behind. To Lancaster it was beginning to seem that there had hardly been a time recently when he hadn't been closeted here, or with Sloan.

He went on: "I was with Sloan first thing today, filling in what background I could." He was seeking information; the days had gone when liaison with Special Branch was his responsibility. First Conway had horned in, and now McBride had virtually taken over. "I gather he's not much further forward."

"As far as Hearne's links are concerned he hasn't been able to move an inch." McBride pushed an ashtray aside as impassively as a croupier. "This is precisely what I was coming to. As I said yesterday, the most pressing thing at the moment is to try and devise a way of pulling some of the fat out of the fire. That's the whole object of putting Hearne into limbo."

"I've been thinking about this," Conway said. "If it can be done, well and good. It's essential to have a shot at it; I agree with you. But, quite simply, it isn't our job. We aren't in the deception business."

"That doesn't mean we aren't capable of coming up with an idea. I've discussed this with Merton, and—"

"Who the hell's Merton?"

"Perhaps I shouldn't have let the name slip. However, it doesn't really matter. . . . The point is that he has no objection, none whatever. I'm not for one moment suggesting that we ourselves go cloak-and-dagger—"

"So I should hope."

Conway had no time for riddles. It didn't seem to have occurred to him that the Old Man was concerned not only with salvaging what he could of the damage to Roman Candle, but his own reputation as well. Watching McBride, Lancaster understood this clearly; it stuck out a mile.

He leaned forward: "Hearne's most likely contacts, surely, would be in the Russian Embassy here."

Conway snorted. "And we walk up to the front door and ring the bell, is that it? Or do we simply post the stuff to them—marked 'To whom it may concern'? . . . Please, please." He said stubbornly: "This isn't for us, Andrew. This isn't our game. Give it to those who make a business of it."

"That's exactly what I'm proposing." It was rare for the Old Man so obviously to show his frustration. "And for the life of me I can't see what your objection is. All I'm saying is this, and it comes in two parts. First, we should prepare a false dossier on Candle—a series of false dossiers, if you like. We can't deny its existence, but we can distort certain facts and figures. There have been so many modifications, especially during the last year, that they can't have got a clear-cut picture as it is. So we have a chance of seriously misleading them; quite a fair chance, I'd have thought. Are you objecting to that?"

"No," Conway said. "Broadly, I'm in agreement. We've nothing to lose."

"Quite. And in my view this department is as well qualified as any other to tackle the preparation of whatever is decided upon."

Conway heaved his shoulders. "Fair enough."

"Then—this is my second part—we should see whether we can't put a worthwhile suggestion Merton's way."

"Why not leave it to him?"

Lancaster asked: "What sort of idea had you in mind, sir?"

"Something quick, obviously. Time's at a premium."

They sat in silence for a while. The hoarse cry of the newspaper seller on the corner below reached them through the uneven rumble of traffic. "Extra. . . . Read all about it. . . ." But for them there was no other crisis, and Lancaster doubted whether the Old Man even heard. He was intent on one thing, one thing only, rolling a pencil between his palms as he concentrated.

Conway was the first to speak. "Yesterday you were talking about the war. Well, during the war a ploy was used which to say the least, was bloody effective."

"Go on."

"This was in Calcutta. Two separate parties had been put into Burma and both had been picked up by the Japanese. It was some while before this was known and for several weeks, under duress, the radio operators sent back totally corrupt information. But when the penny dropped with us counterplans were made. There was a Bengali in the Calcutta jail under sentence of death for murder. He was taken out, fitted with a parachute that wouldn't open, equipped with a radio, flown over Burma and, putting it bluntly, pushed. The Japs found his body and the set, used the codes, and were then fed with precisely what we wanted them to know."

The Adam's apple bounced in the Old Man's scraggy throat. "That was quick, certainly," he said with distaste.

"What's more, the situation we're in now isn't all that different."

"You aren't seriously suggesting—?"

"Of course not. To start with, hanging in this country is out. And war's war; anything goes. But you wanted ideas, and all mine go back to when killing people was encouraged."

Lancaster looked at Conway. So that was the kind of thing he'd done. Those flat brown eyes, like used coins; yet watchful, swift to anger.

"Let Merton—whoever he may be—handle the ins and outs," Conway insisted. "He'll have tricks in plenty up his sleeve. We can prepare the parcel, certainly. But the experts are the ones to work out how it ought to be delivered, and where. Even if Hearne begins to unburden himself it's going to be a damned wily business." He rose. To no one in particular he said: "I can't get used to the idea at all."

"Something needs to be done." This was McBride. "Every day counts."

"Not that. Hearne . . ." Conway stared moodily across the room. "It beats the bloody band."

As if he were aware that Conway was beginning to dominate him again, McBride said in a firm voice: "I'd still like you both to give your minds to possible courses of action. This whole disaster is very much our responsibility."

"We should have tightened our security long ago," Conway retorted, sniping at Lancaster. "For a member of the staff to be able to walk out of here at will with—"

"Yes, I know, George." The Old Man wasn't going to be sidetracked. "David," he said, "I want you to start work on preparing a dossier. Drop everything else. Concentrate on the areas where Adler was weakest—George will help you there—and on those where there has been an excess of modification. Draw on all the Roman Candle data over the last six to eight weeks from Woomera, Guildford, Research and Development and the Liaison Section. Cook the books, in fact. Manufacture another case history based on the most plausible imaginary changes of performance and/or policy. You can't go too far back, remember, but I should have thought you can start somewhere just prior to what Hearne had in his possession."

"I'll do my best."

"Dansie will be informed that you're having unrestricted use of the strongroom with my approval, for research purposes. Right? And, of course, there will be an official staff notice circulated to the effect that Hearne has been seconded, short-term, to Washington, Tyndall taking over his desk in his absence. I'll speak to Tyndall myself about—"

His buzzer sounded and he picked up the black telephone. "Thank you," he said, then transferred to the green one. "Good afternoon. . . . Scramble? Yes, now." He pressed the stud. "Right. Go ahead." And listened. Eventually, he nodded. "Thank you," he said again. "Yes, completely understood. Yes, I'll see to that."

When he hung up his gaze moved from Conway to Lancaster, though when he spoke he was looking at neither. "Hearne's being charged privately at Bow Street later today."

Lancaster's scalp seemed to shrink. "What with, sir?"

"Under Section 1 of the Official Secrets Act. He can be kept on ice for a week, anyhow. But the balloon will have to go up then. So we are only going to have that long in which to act."

Catherine was seeing her aunt again. "She's not too well, David. Forgive me. She asked if I'd come over and I couldn't very well refuse."

[ 164 ]

"Dinner's scrubbed—is that what you're saying?"

"You do understand?"

"Of course. But I've a grudge against this aunt of yours. Particularly as the weekend's off, too."

"Oh no."

"Oh yes. McBride's asked me to undertake some special research for him."

"Over the weekend?"

"I'm afraid so, darling."

"At home?"

"No. Out of town."

"When do I see you, then?"

"Monday."

"I might have expected something like that from Conway. But McBride—he needs his head seen to."


Lancaster stopped at a post office on his way to Chelsea and sent a telegram to Fletcher. *Coming Sunday afternoon.* That was all. No sender's name; a false one on the back of the form. Never before had he contacted Fletcher at the farm, but there were a few last risks to be taken and Fletcher must share them. Then he went to Bramerton Street. Everything had fallen into his lap. He was in a position to capitalize on the Old Man's rescue operation. "We haven't long, David. This dossier—would you make a start on it over the Saturday and Sunday? I'll arrange access for you to the office and the strongroom. You'll be undisturbed then. . . ." Trust had always been McBride's weakness, and anxiety to redeem himself had given Lancaster an unimagined opportunity.

When he slept that night he twitched like an animal.

"You were also at the house, weren't you?" Hearne shouted as if in an echo chamber. *"Weren't you?"* But even before the dream went out of him Lancaster knew it was only a dream. He was safe, safe again. And the real nightmare was almost over.

# Chapter 11 ]

**H**E searched the morning's *Telegraph* and *Mail*, but there was no mention of Hearne. Sloan had pulled it off, then. Nothing in the Court Register, nothing for prying eyes. Hearne would probably be at Brixton and, if Blake was any precedent, even the Governor wouldn't know the details of the charge.

By arrangement with the permanent security-patrol staff Lancaster was let into the office at nine. The lift wasn't functioning, so he had to walk up. The heat wasn't on, either, and the place felt chilly. As a precaution he locked the Weapons Coordination door from the inside, then opened the strongroom and took out all the files he needed. Until noon he concentrated on what McBride was after. By altering the last Woomera launching report he was able to produce an entirely logical chain reaction of error, each comparatively minute but each in turn providing an opportunity for further variation from the true facts. Certain things were basic and couldn't sensibly be tampered with—power plant, category of warhead, overall control system. But there was ample scope for juggling with the cluster-separation technique, laser effectiveness, stabilizers, fuses and nose cone, and thereby falsifying Roman Candle's performance as well as indicating future experimental trends which were totally at variance with reality.

The pattern itself wasn't difficult and Lancaster worked fast. The real problem was in fabricating a dove-tailed series of plausible interdepartmental reports which conveyed both the evolution of incorrect information and the technical changes which flowed from them. It was McBride he had to satisfy, McBride he was fooling. Already the deception was doomed. But wholehearted cooperation was his continuing safeguard.

Sharp on twelve he discontinued preparing the dossier and extracted from the files all the data as yet not passed to Fletcher. Then he replaced the files in the strongroom, locked it, slid the papers he wanted into a large manila envelope and let himself out of the office, the envelope held by his left arm under his jacket. He was quite without qualms; the tailing was off and once again he'd been given carte blanche. McBride wasn't the only one in the salvage business.

He merged into the careless Saturday crowds and made his way to the Strand. The shop he entered sold cameras and photographic equipment, but it also had a stationery counter and, behind turntable racks of bawdy greeting cards, a coin-operated Docustat machine. A small boy separated himself from his mother to watch the machine being used, but he was too young to cause concern. Only when the woman came to retrieve him did Lancaster deliberately block her view of the gray copy edging from the slot: *Department of Research and Development, Weapons Division.* . . .

"Come *on*, Michael, for heaven's sake. And don't stare so.

The man's doing something private. . . . *Michael!*" She caught Lancaster's eye and grinned. "Terrors aren't they, kids?"

He'd never used this shop before; had never used anywhere more than once. When possible he had carried the information in his head, but there was too much of it now —twenty-three sheets of yellows, Round Robins, drawings, reports; so much that he ran out of the right-sized coin and had to go to the counter for change.

"Looks like you're on a shipping order over there, mister," the man said. "Doing its stuff all right?"

"Fine, thanks," Lancaster nodded.

No qualms even then. He was off the hook. No one was going to tour the places where this sort of copying service was available and produce a picture of him, asking: "Do you recognize this man?" And there was no more fear of strangers suddenly closing in, of never knowing whose knock was at the door. He had gone beyond all that—by the skin of his teeth. Even so, he was glad to leave. And once outside he returned the envelope under his jacket; caution would harness him to the last.

He did without lunch and returned immediately to the office building. "When will you be finishing tonight, sir?" the gray-haired patrolman inquired, checking Lancaster's pass for the second time that day.

"About five, I expect."

"And you'll be coming in tomorrow?"

"For the morning, yes."

He walked up and put the lock on the outer doors. He'd been given four extra keys: the department's, Dansie's office and the two for the strongroom. All the other doors were locked, Hearne's included, and it gave him an ugly feeling to pass that particular room. It was uncanny, anyhow, to be in there alone; so quiet. And the quiet somehow suited the tense Sloan had used when referring to Stephen: Was Hearne this? Did Hearne that? . . .

He carried on right through the afternoon, drafting in longhand the first few bogus reports, sometimes amused by his own ingenuity. Once approved they would have to be typed, correctly set out on differing machines; but that could wait. This was McBride's idea, his baby, so let the instructions come from him. One could be too clever, too knowing. By a quarter past five Lancaster had completed about half of the necessary drafts. He was hungry by then, a bit light in the head, and decided to call it a day. Everything except the manila envelope he stacked in the strongroom, used all the keys in turn, then went down to the lobby, his raincoat on this time, the envelope hidden from view.

"Good night, sir," the patrolman said.

There was a chill in the air and the Trafalgar Square fountains swayed in the gusty breeze like glittering weeping willows. Lancaster took a taxi to the West London Air Terminal and booked a midday Sunday flight to Dublin, an evening flight back; 12:15 and 22:10. That done he went home to Bramerton Street, placed the envelope under the mattress, then rang McBride before going out to eat.

"Ah, David. . . . How has it gone?"

"Very well. At least, I hope you'll think so. I ought to finish tomorrow."

"Splendid . . . splendid."

\*　　\*　　\*

He was through by eleven next day, rushing the last few pages, the final one a supposed note from the Minister reluctantly authorizing further expenditure on alternative ground-deployment methods—"the existing method having proved both cumbersome and unreliable, particularly in difficult terrain . . ." He'd cooked the books, all right; and skillfully, too. Nothing overemphasized, nothing too extreme, but the whole acceptably misleading, enough to undermine much of what had already reached other hands. McBride couldn't hope for more, couldn't expect to put the clock right back. But those eighteen pages ought to be sufficient to satisfy, and delude, him. And the remedy was at Lancaster's fingertips, the manila envelope pressed flat between his body and his undervest.

He had parked the Spitfire in Northumberland Avenue. Traffic was light and he used the fast lane almost all the way from Hammersmith on. He was at London Airport with twenty minutes to spare, in time for a quick double. The Aer Lingus Viscount wasn't full and no one sat with him. When they lifted off he leaned back and closed his eyes, remembering Catherine and the journeys with her, the first time, other times, thinking of Fletcher and what had to be said.

He was getting out—now. Yes, now. It was impossible to continue. He'd survived, but only just; twice he'd survived and he couldn't risk a third time. Weapons Coordination was red hot and the whole place was about to be turned upside down. But everything was in the envelope, a bonus if ever there was one. Everything, up to date; drawings, documents, data; the lot. And there was something else Fletcher must pass on—a warning about McBride's intended rescue operation. Details? He didn't know. But it would be launched during the next few days, that much was certain. So tell them—fast.

*Them . . .*

"Never approach us direct. On no account—is it understood?" In Green Park, under the dripping trees that day. "Always contact this address, this man."

Good-bye, Fletcher. Tell them my hands are tied. They've had Roman Candle on a plate, from A to Z. And tell them not to ditch me, because if they try I'll do the same to you. . . .

With a kind of bravado Lancaster rehearsed his piece. A stewardess touched him on the shoulder and handed him a questionnaire to complete. Control had always been one of his assets, yet he started. Perhaps fear would never quite go, even with freedom, even with Catherine.

He studied the form. Against "Reason for Visiting the Republic of Ireland" he wrote: "Business." He was on his way to see about the sale of the cottage. Always have an answer ready, always—even now, especially now.

They were down on time, down in bright sunlight, greeted by the same fitful breeze. The customs was a formality. "Nothing?" the man checking the exit door asked. "No luggage at all?" Lancaster crossed the foyer to the car-hire firm. The red Volvo was special, something he'd managed to arrange months ago; but he didn't want it now. A Vauxhall would do nicely. Around Kilvarna the Volvo would have announced his presence as surely as if he'd entered the Lake Hotel. And he wasn't doing that, or stopping off at the cottage. He was going to the farm; only the farm.

The outskirts of Dublin built up, slowed him, petered out. He swung west and put his foot down. With luck he could make it by five. The countryside rushed past, the hedge-rows blurring, smeared with brown, the hills and flat expanses wheeling beyond. Maynooth, Edenderry, Tullamore, Athlone, Ballinasloe. He knew them by heart. Three years he had been coming here. Then the narrow, twisting back roads with occasionally tinkers' caravans pulled into the verge, or sheep being driven, or solitary people trudging God knows where.

By ten to five he was through Monivea. Not so far now, but it would have taken him over the reckoned-on three hours. And there was still the drive back to connect with the return flight. So he couldn't spare Fletcher long. But then it wouldn't need long. He wasn't coming to argue. Fletcher didn't control him. No one did. He was a volunteer, an amateur, among the best they'd probably ever had, and he was through.

He forked left at the next sign—Kilvarna 6. The farm was to the south of the village and once before he'd approached it this way, in Walker's time. Otherwise, if there was no crisis and word of mouth would do, he and Fletcher had met openly; secrecy sometimes defeated itself. A few minutes together often sufficed. Fletcher had scared him, though. Not his physical bulk, not his surly anger; but his tongue. Time and again this had seemed to threaten everything. "You can trap a man who boasts," Colonel Gray had pontificated back in the Inter-Services Security days. And yet Fletcher had survived—a link, a stranger, someone easy to hate; a domineering, red-eyed lout. "What d'you do, young lady? Or aren't you a working girl?"

When was that? Only a week ago? The time between had seemed endless, yet the memory rankled.

The farm buildings nestled against a slope; a windbreak of conifers hid the house from the road. Fletcher had been there for years; six or seven, it was said. Lancaster turned through the roadside gate and bounced over the track. It was a largish farm. Jerseys were slumped amid the lush grass of the adjoining pasture and a herdsman was coming through from the one next across with a dog. Lancaster ran the Vauxhall onto the concrete tongue protruding from the stone garage and walked stiffly around to the front of the house. Fletcher had probably been on the lookout for him: Sunday afternoon, the telegram had said, and this was on the late side. Lancaster pressed the bell, suddenly nervous, touching the envelope under his vest for about the twentieth time since leaving London.

No one answered. He pressed the bell again. Then a third time, and stepped backwards over the gravel, looking at the windows, up and down. Odd. . . . The bell was working; he'd heard it ring somewhere in the heart of the house. He tried once more, impatiently now, but with the same lack of response. To hell, he thought, and walked around to the back, into a kind of yard that led past some outhouses on to an untidy garden. He knocked hard on the green door; tried the latch. Nothing. No one, not even the daily woman. But, of course, she wouldn't be there, not on a Sunday . . .

Then it struck him. Fletcher was waiting at the Lake Hotel. There was no sign of the Land Rover. The fool, the bloody fool. This was one thing he hadn't bargained for, and time was short. For a few indecisive moments he remained motionless, then pivoted on his heels and made for the car. As he rounded the house a cow bellowed and he remembered the herdsman. He changed direction and made for the gate that led into the field, vaulted it and jog-trotted across the grass.

"Hey!"

Eighty yards away the man turned, watching him. The cows were all on their feet, lumbering closer together as the black-and-white dog headed them in the right direction. Lancaster broke into a walk, careful not to display anxiety.

"Fine afternoon," the man said as Lancaster drew near. An unshaven gnome of a man, neither young nor old, with a broken brim to his soiled hat, a hazel switch in his hands.

"Where's the nearest telephone?"

"Public one? One for putting the coins in?"

"Yes."

"They have them in Kilvarna. The Post Office, but that's not a Sunday place. And Flanagan's, though he'll be closed today for sure." Farce intruded even now. "Kilvarna's along the road here, you could say three miles. You wouldn't be doing yourself harm by trying the Lake Hotel—"

"Nowhere else? What about on the road?"

"Not between here and Kilvarna." The man rasped his beard stubble. "Come to think of it there's a green box in the square, outside O'Reilly's."

"Nothing the other way?"

"In Athenry; they'll be having them there."

"How far's that?"

"Quite a few miles. But wait now—there's one by the cross-roads this side of Athenry. Not so far. Turn right when you're leaving."

"Thanks."

"Kilvarna's as near, I'd say. And you'd have a choice there —in case of finding one's not working."

"Thanks very much." Lancaster was already going.

"Was it Mr. Fletcher you wanted?"

Lancaster hesitated, toying with a lie. But why else was he at the farm? "That's right," he said.

"Mr. Fletcher's away."

"Away?" It didn't sink in at once.

A cow lowered its horns and made a clumsy run at the dog, which twisted clear. The man saw the movement out of the corner of his creased eyes and shouted: "Lay off! Demented, you are."

"Away?" Lancaster repeated.

"Yes, indeed."

"Since when?"

"Friday. Friday evening."

"Where's he gone?"

"Holiday, I heard. Mr. Fletcher's not one for telling a man much." A hint of dislike, tinged with regret. "Comes and goes, he does."

Friday. . . . Lancaster's brain was racing. Fletcher would have collected his letter on Friday.

"Left a note for Mrs. Coady, saying he was off for a while."

"Mrs. Coady?"

"At the house."

Lancaster nodded. He could see what had happened. Fletcher had gone to ground, warned. There was nothing sinister; no threat, no menace. Caution. But caution could smack of funk. Silently, he swore at Fletcher. The front line was a long way from here.

"You've no idea when he might be back, I suppose?"

"Not a truthful one. But he's never gone much more than a

week. Is there any message you'll be wanting me to pass on?"

"I'll drop him a line."

"That's a thought."

"I may leave it in the house," Lancaster said.

"Why not? Well, good-bye now. It's been nice knowing you."

"Good-bye. And thanks."

Lancaster left him, his mind already made up. He kicked through the grass, railing against Fletcher. He'd never thought Fletcher would duck so low or so urgently.

The smell of dung and straw came on the breeze from the barns and milking sheds as Lancaster vaulted the gate. He wasn't going back to London with the envelope on him; out in the field he'd decided that. It would stay here, hidden, to await Fletcher's return. He could let him know where it was in the usual way.

He retraced his steps to the rear of the house. He could have chosen several places, but he rapidly discarded all but one. There was a lime-caked spade propped against the nearest outbuilding. Inside, stacked on the earth floor, were packing cases, rolls of wire netting, bundles of wooden stakes. Dust powdered everything in the gloom. Cobwebs formed a transparent lid to a tea chest half-filled with pieces of harness. He dragged it away from the wall and hurriedly scooped a hole in the floor. It was soon done, six or seven lifts of the spade. Then he opened his shirt and dragged the envelope out, laid it flat, scraped the soil back, trampled it down and, finally, replaced the chest. Stooping in the doorway he took a farewell glance to reassure himself before leaving. Part of a nation's defense was there, thanks to McBride; a killing. And if such a thing as gratitude existed at the far end of the line it would be appreciated how generously he had bought himself out.

Good-bye, Fletcher. No thanks to you, though.

He walked to the car, a stickiness on his skin where the envelope had pressed for so long. The man in the pasture was idling the cows in and Lancaster waved ambiguously as he climbed into the Vauxhall and drove away. A sense of release filled him. He drove fast until he reached Monivea, where he stopped and quenched a raging thirst with beer. "How's that for a head?" the barman said when he'd finished pouring. "You could trot a mouse across it."

Dusk was quick to thicken. Lancaster stopped twice more on the way east, careful how much he drank but drinking out of relief, feeling freer already, unburdened. In a pub in Ballinasloe the radio was on, and as he drained his glass a singer began:

> "Some were waylaid,
> Some were betrayed,
> But what did it prove?
> I ask you . . ."

He went out into the night air with blackness suddenly in his heart, hands clenched. Everything had been necessary. And he knew how to forget. Unaware, Catherine would help him. Must. But for her he would have survived without any trace of pain.

By nine-twenty he was at the airport, the Vauxhall signed in. Upstairs in the departure lounge he ordered whisky and wrote his directions to Fletcher, taking care to be clear and precise: then, savagely, after mentioning the impending deception, he told him to expect nothing more, that it was over, impossible to continue.

Good-bye, Fletcher. Good-bye, wherever you are.

He addressed the envelope to Lisdoonvarna, bought a stamp and posted it. There wasn't time for dinner, but he ate what they served him over the Irish Sea on the plane, barely tasting it, and drank again. Finished and done with; his father used to say that. . . . Keep pace with McBride, show willing, play along; from now on it could be managed with his arms behind his back.

It was approaching midnight before he was in a taxi and heading for home. The day had seemed everlasting, but the drink kept fatigue at bay. Near Hammersmith he tapped on the glass and impulsively redirected the driver to Holland Park. The steps up to the door seemed steeper than usual and once he tripped. He rang Catherine's bell and waited. *She*'d be there. Not like Fletcher, not like vanishing-trick Fletcher, scared of even the sound of gunfire.

The hall light came on. He heard the catch slide.

"Hallo, darling."

"You," she said. Her face was blurred and his ears were deadened against the intonation. "You." That was all. She was in her dressing gown.

"Were you in bed?"

"Not quite."

He was inside now, inside where he belonged, going up the stairs. A bit tight, but no matter. "You don't mind?"

"Mind?"

"This time of night."

"Of course not. But—"

"I've been working like a madman, darling."

"I know. For McBride. If you recall, that's what came between us the day before yesterday."

"That and your aunt. How's she?"

"Better." She was following him up. "Is the work finished?"

"Finished and done with, yes."

He turned on the landing and reached for her. And her kiss was cool, wonderfully cool; her body too, like ice against a fever.

# Chapter 12 ] ✺

**H**E arrived at the office well before anyone else and removed the Roman Candle dossier from the strongroom. He hadn't been given keys to the other weapons' compartments, otherwise he would have added what there was on Discus to Fletcher's haul, slight and largely theoretical though it was. But with Candle alone he'd achieved more than enough, more than could ever have been expected of him. They would recognize that, surely?

"Morning, Margaret." She was ten minutes late, which was punctual for her. "Have a nice weekend?"

"No," she said firmly and wrenched the cover from her typewriter. Her hair was piled high, like brown candy floss. "Damn," she said. "Oh damn and blast Mondays."

"Like that, is it?"

"Yes, like that."

It was easy to tolerate her glare. She was well off. There had been short-lists until a few days ago, Sloan's and his. Another world was at her elbow. Ignorance like hers was a blessing.

"Charming," he said.

McBride sent for him early. His overcoat was still swinging on its peg as Lancaster entered, so he must have that minute come in. He waited until the thick door was shut between them and Ruth.

"Did you finish, David?"

"Yes, sir. Quite comfortably." Lancaster laid the various keys and the slim folder in front of him. "They're drafts, of course."

"Of course." McBride began flipping the pages through. Presently, he said: "I think George had better go over these; he's more *au fait* with the technicalities. But I'd say you've done awfully well. I'm grateful, most grateful."

"Have you decided on a method of delivery?"

"It's not for me to decide. That's Merton's problem—he runs the transport system, as it were. I can only stress the urgency and try to persuade him that existing routes aren't necessarily the best in this particular case."

Lancaster sucked in air. "They've drawn a blank with Hearne, then?"

"Absolutely. I gather he's proving very stubborn." The Old Man looked up. "I suppose he feels a kind of pride in what he's achieved. What began it, d'you think? What set him off? Was it money—something needed quickly on the side?" He shook his head slowly. "Men often deceive themselves as to their true motives." Then, emerging from his reverie, he added: "His Washington posting is official, as of now. I'm going to have it circulated this morning. Meanwhile I'll ask George to comment on this draft of yours and then get it to the Minister for approval."

He was reaching for the phone as Lancaster left him.

Catherine called him an hour later. "Sorry, but you're wanted." As he entered the outer office she said: "Almost everyone's been through here this morning. I wondered when it would be your turn."

"Patience rewarded."

"Who's the smug one now?"

"How d'you do it?" he asked. "How d'you switch it on?"

"Switch what on?"

"Executive Secretary, Grade One. Sometimes you even fool me. And it's scaring."

"Only sometimes?"

"I hate you."

"I was first with that, remember?"

He opened the door into Conway's room. Conway didn't glance at him, but indicated a chair. The folder was open on the desk.

"How long did this take you?"

"A day and a half."

"It's not bad," Conway said grudgingly. "But you were tripping over yourself toward the end."

"Oh?"

"You got your wires crossed."

"Where?"

"On the separation technique, mainly. A bluff's no use if you leave a hole in it and you've all but done that." He swung the folder around and pushed it toward Lancaster as if it were contaminated. "You've got a supposed Minute there from Research and Development which bears no relation to what went before in a Round Robin circulated by the Liaison Section." He waited while Lancaster studied the pages concerned. Some time elapsed. "D'you see what I mean?"

"I think so."

"You've made an assumption. The line you've taken is

plausible enough, but something more's needed—a post-script from the Liaison Section to give Research and Development a reason for their Minute. . . . Get me?"

Lancaster nodded. Conway was right. "That's easily remedied."

"And I also feel we could do with a sketch."

"Possibly."

"There's something else. The Minister's note at the end will need rewriting. The gist of it's fine, but it's not his style. I've made some comparisons—and they will, too." *They* . . . "They'll be as wary of all this as can be, like dogs at a first meeting." Conway leaned forward and retrieved the folder. "Otherwise it's a very fair piece of work."

Bloody schoolmaster. "D'you want me to alter the note?"

"I'll do it. I'll also get a sketch made, if that's possible without someone raising an eyebrow. Perhaps Merton—Merton, isn't it?—will help there. You mock up the additional Round Robin."

"Okay."

"Then, assuming we've had clearance, the stuff needs to be properly presented. We can use the office machine when it comes to copying, but first the originals have got to look the genuine McCoy." Conway paused. "McBride's set on this, you know."

"I know."

"What do you feel about it?"

Lancaster shrugged. It was almost unique for Conway to ask his opinion. "If it works, well and good. You said yourself we've nothing to lose."

"It's not having knowledge of Hearne's channels that worries me. What's here"—Conway tapped the folder—"is reasonable enough. Cleverly delivered, at the very least it ought to have them at sixes and sevens. But I can see them smelling a rat if we aren't damned smart. And time's against us. Hearne's been remanded until Saturday, so we've only five days' grace. Then everything goes sky high —his so-called Washington posting, the lot. Not only will they know their golden goose won't be laying again, but they'll realize we knew it in advance and covered him up. Against that, Adler's information indicated a not inconsiderable time lag between starting point and finish. Everything was at least a week in the pipeline; perhaps more. So if only this stuff can be delivered in acceptable fashion it might get by."

"Why should Hearne have changed his delivery methods?"

"Panic?" Conway suggested. "Anyhow, don't ask me. It's catch as catch can, this business. For specialists. I keep telling McBride it isn't our pigeon, but he won't listen. He feels personally responsible and—well . . . he always did have the Minister's ear." Pique was showing. "And, of course, with his leaving at the end of the year this is do or die for him."

Lancaster held his tongue. Play safe, play along. The real job was done; the rest was a game. Let someone else be desperate now.

Conway said grimly: "If I were dealing with Hearne I'd roast the bastard. We'd have a lead then. But that's not the way things are handled these days."

"D'you want me any more?"

"No, but I'd like that piece from you as soon as possible. Before noon at the latest."

"You'll have it."

* * *

Lancaster lunched alone. On his way back, by St. Martin-in-the-Fields, he bought a midday paper. He knew there would be no mention of Hearne, yet he looked for one when he reached the office; looked for Adler, too, glancing from page to page as if in need of proof that there had been a beginning to all this. But, inevitably, there was nothing. The only name to single itself out was that of Albert Chance. He frowned, remembering. MERCY PLEA REJECTED, the headline read. DEATH SENTENCE ON BRITISH SEAMAN STANDS. Then the paragraph under a Bordeaux dateline: *Albert Chance, 28-year-old British merchant seaman, who was sentenced to death in July for the murder of a local businessman and his family in their house on the city outskirts here, has had his appeal for clemency dismissed by the President of France. The Ministry of Justice states that Chance's execution has been fixed for October 20.*

Lancaster folded the paper and placed it alongside his blotter. Routine intervened, but perhaps half an hour later he read the item again, then ringed it around. Unbidden, an idea was forming, merging with something Conway had mentioned the other day, an idea that began to nag at him as the afternoon wore on. He tried to lose it, to push it aside, but it persisted.

Albert Chance . . . the irony hadn't diminished.

He doodled, thinking. "A lot of things will have to be stretched from now on, George. . . ." The Old Man wouldn't entertain anything as extreme as this. Yet it was something to offer, something to show that he was as determined to redeem the situation as anyone else. And in so doing he would further strengthen his own position: the guilty didn't plan their own defeat.

He rang Conway late in the afternoon. Conway was the one to go to. McBride he had outmaneuvered, and could have done so in his sleep. But with Conway this could be a kind of insurance against that built-in distrust.

"I'd like to see you for a moment."

"Is it important?"

"I think so."

"You'd better come now, then."

Catherine was leaving Conway's room as he went in. "Good afternoon, Mr. Lancaster." She was better at this than he could ever be; her glance was devastatingly impersonal.

"Yes?" Conway said as soon as they were alone.

"It's about delivering the package."

"Yes?"

Lancaster handed him the newspaper. "There's a person here who might possibly help."

"Who?"

"Chance. Albert Chance. Bottom right-hand column."

Conway read the paragraph. "This fellow?" Mystified, he said: "Are you off your head?"

"I hope not."

"You'd better explain. I don't get it. He's due to be executed."

"Precisely."

"I still don't follow." A few seconds' rereading. Then, irritably: "Can't you come to the point? I'm not exactly in a guessing mood."

"D'you remember what you said last week about that wartime ploy in Calcutta? Using someone out of the local jail?"

"I do, yes. But what's that—?" Conway broke off in mid-sentence. His expression was suddenly one of dawning astonishment. "This seaman Johnny? Are you suggesting—?"

"For what it's worth."

"You can't be serious."

"Why not?"

Conway stared at him. "Because," he began, then looked at the paper again. "Because of about every reason under the sun."

"McBride asked for suggestions."

"Practical ones."

"This struck me as a possibility. I don't rate it higher than that. But I thought it worth putting forward."

"You haven't discussed it with him?"

"No."

"Why come to me, then?" An early-warning grittiness in the voice. "You're his blue-eyed boy, after all."

"I wanted to sound you out."

Conway grunted.

"And because," Lancaster added, "the thing stemmed from you in the first place. I can see the snags—"

"Snags!" Conway echoed. "My God!"

"And the objections. But it depends on what's in the balance, and to my mind it could be argued that Roman Candle outweighs them all. It's not only you and McBride who feel the responsibility of what's happened. Internal security in the department has been my charge, you know." Lancaster paused, stifling a sudden memory of Hearne. Adler's ghost was laid, but another had taken its place. "However, there's obviously no point in discussing this idea if you feel it's absolutely out of the question."

He was going to leave it there. He'd played his card, and played it well, he thought. So he leaned across the desk to retrieve the newspaper, intending to go. But Conway checked him.

"Wait a minute. Listen," he said. "To attempt to repeat a wartime thing like that one just isn't possible in this day and age." He began counting off on his fingers. "One, because it stinks. Two, because this fellow Chance isn't our property. Three, because the French wouldn't cooperate. Four, because you can't start parachuting bodies behind the Curtain. Five, because somebody would have to authorize the whole kaboosh; and I can't see any peacetime politician in this country dirtying his hands with it. I could probably give you others, but five good reasons are plenty."

Lancaster had meant to say no more; if there was any merit to be earned from this it was already his. Yet he remarked: "I hadn't thought of him being parachuted."

"How does he get there, then?"

"On foot?" Lancaster shrugged.

"Over the border, you mean?"

"I haven't gone into details. It was the general—"

"He'd need to be dead on arrival."

"Presumably."

"And yet he walks across?" Conway produced his rare, thin-lipped smile. "You want jam on it, Lancaster."

"When he'd almost crossed the strip he'd be picked off from our side."

"My God," Conway exclaimed. "You're a murdering so-

and-so and no mistake." He looked at Lancaster for what seemed a long time. Yet there was no hostility. "You'd authorize that, would you? If you were in the ultimate 'Yes' or 'No' seat you'd give it your approval?"

"Considering what's at stake." Lancaster had never imagined he'd be taken this far. Conway seemed to be drawing the answers out of him, making him overeager to please. "He's a dead man already, anyhow. Your Bengali was, too. The principle's the same."

A snarl of brakes sounded below. Conway glanced down at the circled paragraph with the Bordeaux dateline, and Lancaster could see that he was nibbling.

"Isn't it?"

"Mr. Albert Chance, God help him, isn't under our jurisdiction. And besides," Conway said thoughtfully, "why should a stranger try and cross the frontier somewhere with a load of information on him? A stranger to those beyond the Curtain, I mean. They'll have their delivery boys listed."

"Not being in the bluffing line I wouldn't know. But when someone's blown, or a link's broken, emergency measures obviously have to be taken."

"Hearne could have chosen to employ an outsider, a mercenary; is that what you're saying?"

"After a fashion."

"Because the pressure was on him?"

"I suppose so."

"Then why didn't he try to cross himself? That's what they'll ask themselves over there."

"Maybe he couldn't. Maybe he realized he was under surveillance and dared not risk leaving the country. . . . Anyhow, it's for the experts to paper the cracks."

"Why we're pursuing this I can't imagine. McBride wouldn't touch it with a forty-foot pole. And the French wouldn't even if he did. And it would never get that far because the Minister would run a political mile as soon as it was put to him." Conway pressed his knuckles against his lips. "There's something in it, though . . . Christ, yes."

Even then Lancaster thought it bound to come to nothing.

"What happens to Chance?" Conway asked.

"Happens?"

"How's he executed?"

"Guillotined, I imagine."

"Nowadays?"

"I believe so."

Conway said: "I don't know about you, but I reckon I'd prefer to be shot." Eyes narrowed, he didn't seem to expect a reply. He was niggling at his knuckles with his small, white teeth. "I wonder . . . I wonder if the French *might* be persuaded . . . ?"

There was satisfaction in having him in one's camp, even temporarily; this was the most Lancaster had hoped. But Conway was always on the lookout for an opportunity to show strength and to take unpalatable actions. Most of all he liked to be proved right in the end, and what they were discussing was basically his idea. With it he could demonstrate that a new ruthlessness was necessary. With it he could help the Old Man to his feet, and score off him at the same time. A twenty-million-pound weapon was on the skids and it should never have happened; wouldn't have happened if he, Conway, had been responsible. Scruples, hesitancy, drift— these were no good. Fire had to be fought with fire.

Observing him, Lancaster took his measure. Conway was seeking a merit mark for himself now.

"I'll have a word with McBride."

"When?"

"Right away, if possible." Conway reached for the telephone. "Check if McBride's free, will you?" He shoulder-propped the receiver loosely against his ear and waited, staring at the newspaper, fingers drumming. Perhaps half a minute later Catherine said: "Yes, he's available," and Conway hung up.

"No time like the present."

"Shall I come?"

"Better not." Conway measured Lancaster with a look, as if raising the combative barriers again. "No, I fancy I can bring heavier guns to bear than you." He collected the newspaper from the desk, then paused on his way to the door.

"It says here that Chance murdered a local merchant and his family. How many does that mean? Three? Four?"

"Four, I think. He broke into the house, as far as I remember, intending to rob, then went berserk when he was discovered. . . . I don't see that it matters, though. You'll never persuade McBride on those grounds. This isn't a case of the punishment fitting the crime."

Conway raised an eyebrow. "Are you back-pedaling, by any chance?" He was unconscious of the pun.

"Of course not," Lancaster retorted.

Yet he was; a small part of him was. Suddenly, at that moment. He followed Conway through the outer office into the corridor and Catherine's glance as he passed was again intent upon appearances. "You're hard," she'd said. "Under-

neath you're as hard as nails." He'd never forgotten that remark; it framed what he was beginning to recognize in himself. Dedication, purpose—he had had them once and now
they were fading. And in the process of getting out, of assur-
ing his salvation, he was the mainspring of something that,
even if there were no other secrets, Catherine would never
forgive him for if she knew.

He entered his own room. Margaret was already packing
up. Was it that late? "I'm off now," she said presently. "Good
night, Mr. Lancaster." Take it or leave it. He watched her
go, and brooded, deep in melancholy. God, he thought, if
only there could be no more lies, no more victims; if only he
could be free of the terrors that occasionally possessed him.
Eventually he cleared his desk and deposited his boxes in
the strongroom. It was six-thirty by the time he left. McBride
joined him in the lift and they rode down together, alone.

"George Conway's been to see me."

"I know."

McBride looked grieved, and as frail as he ever had, like
a man whose friends were all in their graves.

"I gather," he said as if it were a complaint, "that this suggestion originated from you."

"In a way, yes."

"I never expected you'd be one to abdicate your conscience, David."

It was curious to be encouraged by a reprimand. McBride
had killed the idea, then; killed it stone dead, as Lancaster
had felt certain he would. So the limit had been reached after
all.

# Chapter 13 ] ❧

**B**UT in the morning the idea was still very much alive. To Lancaster's surprise, when McBride summoned him Conway was already there and Chance was the subject of heated discussion. He could feel the atmosphere as he went in. Conway was in his pacing mood; the Old Man occupied the swivel chair. Except for a brief silence neither of them acknowledged his arrival, and Conway, who seemed to have been interrupted in mid-sentence, continued with: "Was it so unreasonable?"

"Certainly it was."

"Well, I'm sorry. But it seemed—"

"*I'm* directly responsible to the Minister." McBride's tone was of icy indignation. "And you were well aware of my views on this particular matter."

"Yes, but—"

"It isn't pleasant to have someone go over one's head. You'd be the last person to tolerate such a thing."

"Look, Andrew, I've apologized. I'm sorry." Conway was clearly hating this, all the more so with Lancaster present. "But the fact that the Minister didn't send me packing bears out my contention that the Chance business has possibilities."

McBride opened his mouth to speak, but dried.

"What other suggestions have been made?" Conway demanded. "From what you tell me Merton is worried about using existing channels either because they are unsuitable for this type of operation or because they're in a tricky state of health. All right; I accept that. We can't insist on barging in if we're likely to jeopardize anything. But we can, and we must, give serious consideration to any idea that seems likely to work. *Any* idea. What's more, we'd be fools not to try and carry others with us. Chance *can* be used, and effectively. This isn't a time to be squeamish."

"It would be murder."

"No."

"You say no, I say yes," McBride countered.

"And I say you're splitting hairs. He's going to be executed in any case."

"By another country, according to their laws." McBride seemed suddenly to remember Lancaster's existence. "Do you consider I'm splitting hairs, David?"

Alert, watchful, slightly ill at ease, Lancaster turned the question. "I missed what you've been saying earlier. Has the Minister given his approval?"

Conway answered. "He didn't commit himself either way. His attitude was about fifty-fifty."

"George went to see him last evening—privately." McBride's expression conveyed that, to his mind, there was no loyalty left. "After I'd quite categorically stated that I, for one, wanted no part in anything so . . . so . . ." He searched vainly for a word, then gave up. "This department has enough to answer for as it is."

"I don't get it," Conway said angrily. "We've gone to immense trouble to cover up Hearne's arrest. When I say 'we'

[ 195 ]

I don't simply mean Weapons Coordination; I'm talking about all those concerned. And the breathing space has been used to produce a first-rate technical decoy"—a glance toward Lancaster—"which, incidentally, has received official blessing. So where's the point if we sit on our backsides and let the opportunity go to waste? Hearne might as well have been charged in open court and we could have written Roman Candle off as a badly maimed item in our armory and concentrated on seeing to it that a leak of this dimension, a leak of any kind, never happens here again. . . . I was against dabbling in the deception game, remember? You were the one who insisted that some sort of retrieving action was essential, that we ought to put our heads together—right? Well, Lancaster and I have done that thing."

"Indeed you have. And let me remind you exactly what your proposition is. This man Chance is to be taken to the East German frontier, let loose like a coursing hare and then shot. Am I correct? Shot in cold blood?"

"The French will execute him in cold blood."

"Legally." McBride again addressed himself to Lancaster. "What you've suggested is atrocious, David. Utterly atrocious. . . . Thank God the French wouldn't wear it."

"Don't be so sure," Conway said. "Provided there's some quid pro quo, they might. Whatever else the French may be, they're realists. If there's something worthwhile in it for them on the side—"

"We're talking about a man's life."

"A man's death, Andrew."

A pigeon lifted off the windowsill behind McBride's desk as if in terror.

"A man's death," Conway repeated, "which can be put to

some use instead of being totally valueless." He was very much on the attack now. "Even the Minister saw that."

"Thank you," McBride said acidly. "I must say you choose your words to splendid effect."

Conway shrugged. "If we're going to be emotional about Mr. Chance we might as well drop the subject. When Lancaster first put the notion forward my reaction was much the same as yours. But the more one thinks about it the more it seems to offer a practical solution. Hell, it's already Tuesday. The Candle stuff is as good as ready. What other scheme is there? If I were in your shoes I'd press for this to be put in train. I'd argue until I was blue in the face that here's a unique way of feeding the wrong information back in the time remaining to us."

McBride said with contempt: "I don't deny it's unique." He paused for several seconds. "Not only is it that, but it provides no guarantee of delivery."

"Of course it does."

"Oh? Well, what happens if your messenger boy, as you charmingly termed him yesterday, decides not to cross over when you've taken him to the frontier?"

"He'd be crazy not to," Conway said. "What would you do?" He failed to catch McBride's eye, so looked at Lancaster. "You're a dead man, remember, and someone says 'There you are. Freedom. Off you go . . .' You'd grab at it, wouldn't you?"

"I reckon so."

"I damned well would. One chance in a hundred is better than none at all."

"How, then," McBride asked, "would you make certain he doesn't finish up on the other side, safe and sound, and thereby blow your operation to smithereens?" All the time he kept saying "your," stressing it. "How would you remove that one chance?"

"By employing the best available marksmen," Lancaster replied.

To quibble now would serve no purpose. He could afford McBride's censure. McBride hadn't much longer to go, anyhow; in under three months he wouldn't be sitting there. And though Conway would never be less than dangerous, his teeth were drawn for the time being. He had become a confederate, intent on a private satisfaction. Whereas the Old Man would forgo his retiring knighthood rather than soil himself. "*Your* scheme . . . *Your* messenger boy . . ." And everything was on his side. Albert Chance would go to his end in the way the French saw fit, despite anything Conway might say or do, no matter how many back doors he tried. Yet Conway was the one to back, the one to stand by. Chance was a distraction, pushing Hearne and the case against Hearne into the background. Let McBride have his conscience. The game of trying to salvage Roman Candle had entered an ugly dimension, but to Lancaster it remained fantasy, a means of putting the seal on saving his own skin.

Fletcher had been fed, gorged. That was the one reality. All this about Chance would come to nothing.

"Let me put it to you another way," McBride said quietly. "Say you were one of these marksmen, what then?"

"But I wouldn't be."

"What I'm asking—what I'm asking you both—is how you would feel if your own finger was on the trigger, your own eyes actually lining up the sights?"

Conway said brusquely: "You're arguing from a false and an emotional standpoint."

McBride ignored him. "What about you, David? Killing a man wouldn't worry you?"

"That isn't a fair question, sir."

"Why not? You've already set yourself up as judge and jury." He seemed particularly to want Lancaster's view, as if he couldn't yet believe he'd again misread someone close to him. "You're prepared to see a man treated like an animal because of expediency? . . . Murdered?"

With exasperation, Conway flung out: "Chance is already due to be killed, Andrew. . . . Hell, for the last time—"

"Not by shooting. And not for our benefit." Again the Old Man turned to Lancaster, as if in appeal. "You disagree with me?"

"In the circumstances, yes."

McBride swallowed. His glance was withering. "In that case," he said, "you'll no doubt be delighted if the Minister is infected by the idea in the way that George has been. And even more delighted if, by a miracle, the French agree to let us demonstrate just how talented some of us can be in certain directions on this side of the Channel."

He stood up, turning his back on them in disgusted dismissal. In the corridor Conway touched Lancaster on the arm. "And some fell on stony ground."

"What did you expect?"

"Wait and see. The Minister was more willing to listen than I implied. It was more like sixty-forty in our favor." Conway had got the bit between his teeth. But Lancaster didn't believe him.

\* \* \*

Conway rang him later: it was all Conway these days.

"I want you to spare an hour this evening."

"Doing what?"

"Making the copies."

"They pretty well make themselves on that machine."

"I'd rather you were there. You know how the thing functions, and this isn't a time for butterfingers. Stay on after the shutters have gone up, will you?"

It was a quarter past six before Conway came to his office. He had the keys of the room where the Xerox was housed. "All set?" he asked briskly, and they went there together. It was a tiny room, like a cell, without windows. A naked bulb hung from the ceiling. Conway opened the folder he was carrying and spread the contents, sheet by sheet, on the table alongside the machine. Some were foolscap, some quarto. At least three different typewriters had been used.

"Who prepared them?"

"Merton's people. Good, eh? The paper matches, department by department, as well as the type faces, and the way the stuff is set out can't be faulted. . . . You see where I altered the Minister's note?"

Lancaster read quickly. The style seemed much the same to him, but what did it matter? "You've included a sketch, then?"

"Nose-cone insulation, yes. It's a small point, but every little helps to fog the issue, particularly as Research and Development have had so much trouble in that direction." Conway went to the machine. "How d'you get this jack-in-the-box to work?"

"Presto." Lancaster flicked the wall switch. "Who exactly is Merton?"

"McBride deals with him. Keeps him up his sleeve. Odd, you know—McBride. He's as determined as anyone else to try and pull this off. A deception was his brainchild, after all. But when it comes to the pinch he's secretly ashamed and goes all moralistic."

"How many copies?"

"Make it two, just in case Merton or someone has an alternative idea and one's not enough. No, better make three; we can always destroy any spares, and we don't want to fiddle around in here again." Conway watched Lancaster set the machine. "Is that all you need do?"

"Just about."

When the first print was ejected Lancaster lifted it from the tray. "How's that?" A supposed Guildford modification. "All right?"

"Great." Conway nodded approvingly. "Yes, that's damned good. That's bloody good." He spoke as if he had never seen anything like it before. "Perfect."

"You know what will happen?" Lancaster said. "We'll soon be all dressed up with nowhere to go."

"Not on your life. This'll get there."

"In the time?"

"I'm sure of it."

"Not with Chance. McBride will fight that tooth and nail."

"Let him. But it's not in his hands any longer. And I've every reason to think the Minister's taken the proposition further." Conway was always fond of this shadowy talk—the Minister, the P.M.

"You said yesterday that he'd run a political mile."

"So I did, but I misjudged him. More than anyone he realizes Roman Candle is about as valuable to us as a puff of smoke unless something drastic is done. He's no slouch. I reckon he'd willingly drag the gold fillings out of his grandmother's teeth if it were going to help the national security in any way."

"There's still the French."

"Offer them a share in that Trapeze project, say, and they'd give Chance back without any questions asked." A little laugh, like a clearing of the throat. "If you thought it was so impossible why did you put the poor bastard up? You're the one who thought of him as an Aunt Sally."

Conway took charge of the copies when the last one had been made. He returned to his own office with them, presumably to lock them away. Lancaster had never known him so affable, but he wasn't taken in. Conway blew hot and cold as the occasion suited. What was more curious was his confidence in the outcome of the Chance affair. Where this confidence came from, how much of it was a pose, Lancaster couldn't tell. But he was at last beginning to think he might have underestimated him—not as an enemy, but as an accomplice.

"Good night," he called along the corridor, and left. It was almost dark and there was some mist about; a foghorn moaned from the river, filling a lull in the traffic. Lancaster didn't know why, but he associated pain with that sound, pain and fear. He walked to Jerry's; he wasn't meeting Catherine until seven-thirty, so there was no hurry.

"Welcome, Mr. Lancaster," Mario said. "For two, isn't it?"

"That's right."

He ordered a whisky and waited for Catherine to come. Once before, as a result of Norris, he had had the feeling of something happening behind his back, something over which he had no control. He'd been wrong then, but he wasn't this time. Conway was even more confident than he'd admitted; the conviction was growing. There *were* no limits, no rules. Others in addition to Conway had latched on to what had started as a protective suggestion, and Conway was aware to what degree.

Lancaster twirled the glass slowly in his fingers. Christ, he was sick of it all, sick of hunches that deceived, of crudeness and subtlety in every form, of himself. Yes. Hearne had been enough, more than enough.

"Hallo, David."

"How's my girl?" He flashed a smile as Mario assisted Catherine into the banquette.

"Thirsty."

"Campari?"—she nodded, and Mario heard and nodded, too—"and another Scotch, please."

"Certainly," Mario said, going.

"How's it been today?"

"Like a madhouse." Catherine tossed her hair. "Don't let's talk about it. If there's one thing I can't stand it's not being trusted, and I don't know what Conway's doing half the time. What's more, I'm obviously not meant to know."

"I'm the last person to ask."

"You? The Director's personal assistant? Nonsense." She looked at him as if she were finding fault.

"Shop's a bore," he said uncomfortably.

"Diplomat."

"I'll tell you this. You're becoming like a stranger in the office. And I hate it."

"Sorry."

She seemed tired. When he touched her hand there was

no answering pressure, and he looked at her anxiously, fearing that her weariness might also be weariness of him. Vaguely he recalled how wooden she was on his return from Dublin on Sunday—and found an excuse; he'd been a bit sodden then. But now . . . He was used to these retreats of hers, but he wasn't prepared for the pang of alarm. All day he'd waited to bring his loneliness to her and have it stifled. Before, with women, he was able to relieve himself of doubt and fear and anxiety in his own way. With her it was different. But for her he probably wouldn't have cared a tuppenny damn about Albert Chance or Stephen Hearne. She had led him along a road he didn't know and the one thing now, the only thing, was that she should remain there with him.

She brightened as they ate; her smile came more readily. And when he told the story about the Jewess and the steel magnate she laughed herself tearful. But he watched her, both at Jerry's and later in the discothèque, dreading some tell-tale glimpse of discontent, boredom, coolness—he didn't quite know what.

"Happy?" he asked once, cheek to cheek, and the squeeze on his arm was sufficient to ease his doubts.

He took her home, but didn't go in. He would have, but she said good night at the door. And he told himself that he understood. " 'Bye, darling . . ." He had never sought love, but he had found it, and it belonged where Hearne and Chance did not, Walker did not, Sloan and Gilligan did not, Conway did not, Fletcher did not, even the Old Man did not. Yet it overlapped that world and would finally set him free of it. The sooner the better.

He made for Chelsea across Hyde Park through the dark

and the mist, and the foghorn kept sounding mournfully from the direction of Battersea.

Nothing out of the way happened on Wednesday morning. McBride didn't send for him and Conway, according to Margaret, hadn't come in.

She asked Lancaster: "Have you initialed those papers yet?"

"Yes—and one's wrongly addressed. Tyndall's taken over the Army desk."

"So he has. Ah well, I'll alter that. It was sudden, wasn't it, Mr. Hearne transferring to Washington?"

"Very."

"Lucky him."

For a week he had existed in a kind of fever: nothing had seemed entirely positive, most of all the fact that he'd survived. Sometimes in the night he had awakened with a start, wide awake, rigid on his elbows, and been unable to sleep again because of the beating of his heart, thinking, Oh Christ, thinking, alternately scared and troubled, hardly daring to believe that he had done enough or torn by what he'd already done. Then coming here and offering the required expression, the careful answers, nerves and instinct working overtime.

"Lucky? I'll say he is."

He bumped into McBride in the men's room shortly after lunch. "Spare me a minute, will you?" The Old Man said. "There's something you ought to know."

"Yes, sir?" They were in his office now, shut in.

"You'll be pleased to hear, I'm sure, that our people are in active negotiation with the French Ministry of Justice about Chance. The Minister and Merton are over in Paris now."

Conway had been right, then. Things were moving, and moving fast. Lancaster fumbled for a reply. He'd lost ground with McBride, perhaps irretrievably, but it couldn't be helped. He had chosen what must prick him. "As long as Roman Candle is saved from the scrap heap I'm prepared to argue that we're justified."

"You'll have no regrets?"

"Regrets? No."

McBride hummed quietly. "George Conway is over with them."

"Conway? Why Conway?"

"The French," McBride said in a dead tone, dry of all emotion, "want their pound of flesh and George Conway is there to advise the Minister what we might be prepared to offer. The market in international secrets is a dirty business, David, dirty and devious. You should have realized that before you opened your mouth."

There was a photograph of the Minister in the evening editions, not of him boarding a Paris-bound plane, but watching a tank demonstration on the testing ground the previous day. The Brigadier was alongside him, arms folded, jaw jutting as if to ward off any possibility of another fiasco. Lancaster studied the Minister's cadaverous face. It was a bad picture, taken into the light, and the coarse screen was blotched, but the more Lancaster looked at it the more he seemed to be met by the stare of the skull alone. How easy it was to be deceived: the smiling handshake, the baby publicly kissed, the platitudinous declaration. How easy—unless you were in the know . . .

Not a mention of Chance anywhere. And Hearne wouldn't make the headlines until Saturday. Then, and then only, could a door be closed on the past with any certainty.

Back at the Bramerton Street flat Lancaster typed one final note to Fletcher; a postscript. *Re deception. Have every reason to believe a British national, name immaterial, will be used to stimulate West-East crossing attempt before the coming weekend. Decision not yet firm, details not yet finalized. But intention is that he will carry totally false information. This, as already indicated, must be ignored.*

No signature, the phrasing guarded yet crystal clear. Martin Brain c/o Tythe Barn Inn, Lisdoonvarna. . . . Good-bye Brain, good-bye Fletcher. For the last time. Come out of your hole; it's safe now. Go to the shed at the back of the house and move the tea chest. Everything's there. . . .

He would have done that already, surely? If not already, soon. Roman Candle's rescue was doomed even before it was launched, and Chance was doomed anyway.

Lancaster slept, and there were no dreams. Though for a moment when he awoke, just for a moment, he thought he heard a woman sobbing.

Conway was talking about the French. "They're an insular, chauvinistic lot, they really are. And they're so damned mercenary. Asking them a favor is about as optimistic an occupation as asking the Mafia to waive a grudge."

"I don't see what your complaint is," McBride said. "You got what you went for."

"Only, I suspect, because Chance is an embarrassment to them."

"Chance, or the guillotine?"

"Both. They rarely use the thing these days, but Chance qualified on the grounds of murders committed after the perpetration of a felony; that's what the book says. And there was a shocked reaction to the killings which was nationwide."

This was Thursday, the three of them in the Old Man's room, and Conway in full control.

"They'd been softened up by diplomatic exchanges before we got there, but only to a degree. They were still pretty prickly to start with—they being the Minister of Justice, in person, a couple of his link men, Deuxième Bureau, I shouldn't wonder, and the Director of the Defense Office. Four against three, and some of the haggling got on my wick. But the upshot is that we can have Chance in exchange for their being fully briefed on Goldfinch."

Lancaster frowned, temporarily at a loss. "Goldfinch?"

"Antitank weapon, wire-guided—you know the one."

"But that's practically obsolete."

"Obsolescent."

McBride said: "I told you it's a dirty game, David."

"It satisfied them. In any case Goldfinch is an advance on what they're currently using. Far more compact, lighter, and—"

"What George is telling us is that he got a bargain," McBride said stonily. He seemed a passenger now, reduced to carping, Conway's supremacy acknowledged.

"What I don't understand," Lancaster said, "is how the French will explain away Chance's transfer to us."

"They won't have to. They'll go through the motions of

carrying out the death sentence. As far as the world is concerned the law will have taken its course. A burial can be cooked up as easy as pie, a coffin brought over here if that's what the relatives want." Conway spread his hands. "It's all been done before, one way or another; don't let's fool ourselves. Chance becomes our property at ten tonight; twenty-two hundred. From then on Merton's lot takes over."

With sudden firmness, McBride said: "They aren't taking over the Candle material. Oh no."

"The Minister was agreeable."

"To blazes with the Minister. This is a departmental responsibility—my department. And I'm not letting anything so vital out of our hands until the very last moment."

"That's all very well, but—"

"Listen." McBride's gray eyes moved from one to the other. "You decided on the vehicle. And you, George, have arranged for it to be in running order." He selected his words to maximum effect. "All right. We won't go into that again. But I'm telling you that no one else, repeat no one, will have charge of this material until zero hour."

"In that case you'd better speak to the Minister yourself."

"I intend to."

"The way it was left with Merton was that his people would take delivery of Chance in Paris—he's being moved from Bordeaux now—any time after ten P.M. He'll then be flown to the British in West Germany, where arrangements will have been made by the time he arrives. It was more or less assumed that whoever escorts Chance will also have the package."

"Well, it was a wrong assumption. I'm insisting on closer control than that." McBride pursed his lips defiantly, then turned to Lancaster, in the grip of a snap decision. "Is your passport in order, David?"

"I think so."

"Good. I want you to go over, then."

"To Paris?"

"Yes."

"You'll have to clear this with the Minister, Andrew," Conway chipped in.

McBride ignored him. "I'll discover whom you'll need to contact, and where—"

"I can tell you," Conway said. "The fellow's called Sydenham, and—"

"*I'll* brief David, if you don't mind."

Pettiness ill became the Old Man. He moved the blotter needlessly on his desk, as if its position offended him. "If your passport isn't valid we can easily have it attended to." His hands were shaking.

"It is."

"You're sure?"

Lancaster nodded. McBride seemed to be fussing as a means of distracting himself from the real issue.

"Very well. Now look. I'll give you full instructions later. But I can tell you now that your job will be the safe custody of the Roman Candle material. No one else is to touch it, is that understood? No one except you and . . . and Chance."

He spoke the name with reluctance, as if plagued by guilt. It had come to this, his gaze implied; and there was a glint in his eyes which went further, as near to bitter reproof as Lancaster could make out.

"Very well, sir."

# Chapter 14 ] 🐸

A WEEK ago he had been in the house with Nadine, compromising Hearne up to the hilt. Three days ago Chance had earned a single paragraph in the *Standard*. And Fletcher had been sandwiched in between. The week had gathered unbelievable momentum, day by day. Only on Monday Conway had said: "I can give you five good reasons why a scheme like this wouldn't work." And now everything was fixed, a deal done, arrangements made.

The Old Man was still fussing, still hiding from reality behind the details, as if thereby he could somehow maintain a measure of blamelessness.

"The hotel you're to go to is the Alexa, on the Boulevard Magenta. And the person you're to meet is called Sydenham. Sydenham—have you got that?" Conway might never have existed.

"Sydenham, yes."

"You're booked on the five-o'clock flight, arriving Le Bourget around six. He'll expect you any time from about seven on. Ask for him at the desk."

"Right."

"I can't tell you more. He'll have his own instructions from Merton and he'll be liaising with the French and, later, with our people in Germany. Leave all that side to him. Your sole duty will be to see that none of these documents goes astray."

"When exactly do I part with them?"

"When Sydenham parts with Chance."

McBride opened a drawer in his desk. "Here's a special carrying case with a wrist chain." Lancaster knew the kind; Queen's Messengers used them. "We'll load it when you're ready to go. Your ticket will be here then, too. And there'll be a special clearance pass for customs and immigration. Present it in conjunction with your passport and there will be no trouble. The pass is only temporary, mind; you'll have to relinquish it as soon as you return."

"When will that be?"

"Tomorrow. Now, have you any questions?"

"There was some mist about last night. Five might be cutting it a bit fine."

"Make a periodic weather check. You can always transfer to an earlier flight." Trafalgar Square was bathed in weak sunshine, but it had been yesterday. "I'd rather you weren't hanging about overlong in Paris, though. You'll find the case is burdensome enough without having to kick your heels unduly. . . . One more thing. No word to anyone about your journey, David. To no one—understood? Draw what you need from the expenses float. I've signed the form—here. You'll see it merely says 'General Duties.'"

Despite everything, the Old Man hadn't spared himself.

Twice Lancaster looked into Catherine's room, but each time she was with Conway. He went home to collect his passport and to pack a grip—pajamas, underwear, shirt, razor; he'd probably need them. On his way back to Whitehall he took a quick lunch at a cafeteria. He left his grip in the down-stairs lobby when he arrived at the office. There was a damp-ness in the air, like a hint of things to come, but London Air-port reported outgoing flights on schedule.

Catherine was using the telephone when he next put his head around her door. She closed her hand over the mouth-piece: "Conway?"

"You."

Trying to listen at the same time she suggested: "Later?"

"How much later?"

But she dropped her gaze. "I'm sorry," she said quickly into the phone. "Could you repeat that? Research and De-velopment are what? Oh, I see. . . . I'm sorry, but I'm afraid I was distracted. . . . Yes, yes, go ahead."

Lancaster withdrew. A smile would have been something. Perhaps he expected too much. Perhaps it had always been like this here—the demands of others, the drone of traffic, the tramp of messengers. He couldn't remember how it used to be. But a part of him was crying out for an end to restraint, an ever-ready touchstone, repeated proof. Everything was happening at a hundred miles an hour. Paris had been flung at him as a result of the Old Man's obstinacy. Chance had been a name, and he had never imagined it would be any-thing more. Uneasily he returned to his own office. Who was the first to say: "I love you"? And how could she know with what desperation he needed to hear it said again? Or why now, especially now? They shared a single secret: he had dozens, some his alone.

"David?"

"Yes, sir . . . ? Right away."

The Xeroxed copies were in a plastic envelope. McBride

slipped them into the case and handed Lancaster the key; the same key opened the lock on the wrist chain. Air ticket, passport, diplomatic courier's pass . . . and, unexpectedly, two hundred francs. "You'll hardly need more. Our people will look after you in Germany." There was really nothing further to be said. In McBride's eyes, Lancaster knew, he was prime mover and accessory in one; but the Old Man had done with argument. He wouldn't forget and he wouldn't forgive, but there would be no more talk. Everyone must justify this to themselves, wash their hands in their own way.

"Do you want me to contact you at any time?"

"No," McBride said wearily. "No, that won't be necessary. Just do what you have to do."

"Good-bye then, sir."

The familiar nod; that was all. Ruth smiled her duplicated smile as Lancaster went through. His watch showed three thirty-five. He drew an advance from the float, Miss Ayres handing the money over as though it were hers. When he returned, Catherine was in with Conway again; anyway, her room was deserted. "Hallo," Dansie said, bumping into him in the corridor. "Is the lion in his den, or isn't he?"

"Tied up."

The day remained clear, but time was pressing. A cup of tea had gone cold on Lancaster's desk. He sat down, defeated by the inadequacy of words even before he started, and scrawled: *Since lunch there has been a conspiracy against our having more than a few only too normal Weapons Co-ordination exchanges. Can't see you until Friday evening at the earliest. Will telephone as soon as possible. Hate this way of going on. Love you. Need you. Miss you—even from four rooms away. Please, please, do the same. You began this, after all.* He stuck the envelope down and double-sealed it with tape. *Miss C. Tierney. Personal* . . . Her room was still empty when he got there and he wound the envelope under the typewriter roller.

"Are you leaving?" Margaret asked pointedly when he decided he could wait no longer; she, of all people, made it sound like a reprimand.

"That's it," he said, and went. Downstairs, he collected the grip from the commissionaire and clipped the briefcase chain around his left wrist. Slate-gray clouds had obliterated the sun but the weather was holding. He waited on the corner by Admiralty Arch and a cruising taxi was his within minutes.

"London Airport," he said, and settled back, submerged within himself, trying not to think about Albert Chance, or the break-neck speed at which an ingratiating idea had been transformed into action, or the irony that had committed him to follow it through. Trying not to, yet thinking of nothing else. Events had run away with him this time. Walker had been inevitable, Hearne had been necessary. But Chance was neither. Albert Chance was going to grisly waste.

London Airport sank beneath the Trident. There had been a few low-lying scarves of mist along the motorway, but nothing serious.

Lancaster sat with the briefcase in his lap; the grip had gone through with the general baggage. He was accustomed to being surrounded by people whose lives were wholly normal, whose words and laughter proclaimed degrees of innocence he had long since abandoned. He glanced in envy along the tube of the fuselage at their faces: earnest, cheer-

ful, nervous, bleary. What did they know of what was done
to their detriment, done in their name? The world was more
devious, more ruthless, than they could ever comprehend.
The tensions, the gambles, the inner torments that no one
ever penetrated—what did they know of these? How could
they realize that a man might change as he made his way
through the maze, change because he had found a woman,
the woman, and decide on a way out? And, in choosing it,
become involved at close quarters in something that was increasingly repugnant to him?

For what? His fingers tightened on the case. The game
had got out of hand, yet he couldn't draw back. France was
already showing over the curve of the earth's shoulder. He
shut his eyes and let the darkness in, his mind aching for
Catherine. He would purify himself with her, in time.

Le Bourget embodied most of the sameness of all airports
—the same echoing clatter, the same herds being grouped
and shepherded, the same slumped figures waiting, the same
metallic announcements. It was two years since Lancaster
had been there and the place didn't look or sound any different. The pass gave him priority: immigration, customs,
he was cleared without question. By six-fifteen he was heading for the Boulevard Magenta, wincing at the way the driver
handled the wheel. Like any tourist he watched the city offer
itself, drably at first, then by comparison more enticingly,
beginning to sparkle as the dusk thickened. *Paris makes the
pulse beat faster,* a hoarding proclaimed: for Chance? Lancaster thought. What would he have been told, for God's
sake?

They reached the Alexa at ten to seven. It was a two-star

place, not quite seedy. Lancaster paid the taxi off and went in, going immediately to the desk and asking for Sydenham; there seemed no point in waiting. A severe-looking blonde said: "Is Mr. Sydenham staying here?"

"I believe so."

She checked the list with a scarlet fingernail, then lifted a telephone and asked for the room number. "You wish to speak to him?"

"Please."

He took the receiver from her. "Hallo, who's that?"

"John Sydenham."

"This is Lancaster."

"Oh fine. I'll be there right away."

It was a younger voice than Lancaster had somehow expected. He hung up, thanked the girl, and crossed to one of the couches in the foyer, his overcoat draped on his left arm to cover the wrist chain. People were coming and going all the time; the language had changed but normality had no end: the lift hummed up and down. Sydenham used the stairs, emerging into view and looking around as if he were suddenly unsure of his whereabouts. Lancaster had been given no description of him, but the Wykehamist tie was a clue in itself. He stood up, catching Sydenham's eye, extending a hand as they approached each other.

"David Lancaster."

"Hallo. Good trip?"

"As smooth as glass."

Sydenham was medium height, dark-haired, clean-shaven; about thirty, Lancaster reckoned. A pleasant face, on the plump side; hardly an executioner's. No creases, no lines, no hint of inner journeys.

"I expect you could do with a drink?"

"I could, yes. But I'm lumbered with this thing"—Lancaster moved his arm—"and a bar might be a bit public."

"In my room?"

"Okay."

They walked. "Only one floor," Sydenham said. He rang down for two whiskies. Lancaster chucked his coat and grip onto the bed, but continued to nurse the briefcase.

"How much have you been told?" Sydenham asked.

"Not much. No details. My instructions are not to part with what's in here until the last moment. Until then it's going to be follow-my-leader. Wherever you go, I go."

"Well, I'm due at Fresnes at ten sharp."

"The prison?"

Sydenham nodded. "That's the first thing. I collect at the tradesmen's entrance, as it were. But you'd better not come. We'll pick you up afterward, say quarter past."

"Here?"

"Here will do nicely."

"Who are 'we'?"

"The French aren't letting go until they're no longer territorially responsible."

"When will that be?"

"About an hour later. The RAF are flying us out from a strip near Beauvais. *Sans phrase, sans cérémonie.* Once aboard we're on our own."

"And we go where?"

"It was to have been Gütersloh, but that's been changed. Southeast of Hanover is the last I heard. We'll car from there."

"To?"

"Feldhagen. Our ETA is two A.M."

Their drinks arrived. Sydenham found a tip, then watched the door close. "Well, good luck." He said it with an odd smirk, as if the translation had suddenly occurred to him. "There's a smell about this, and no mistake"—and Lancaster wondered how far his knowledge went. "Is what you've got in the case very bulky?"

"Not particularly."

"It would be pointless to ask what it is, I suppose?" Only someone inexperienced would have said that. "It must be right out of the top drawer."

"Let's stick to the interdepartmental distrust thing, shall we?" Lancaster proffered a cigarette. "I wouldn't be here otherwise. And I'd far rather not be, I can tell you. Who do we hand over to at Feldhagen?"

"A Colonel Rouse."

"And then what? Do we make our own way home?"

"They'll see to that."

"They'd better. A generous government allotted me two hundred francs, but nothing for Germany. I'm your guest once we're there. But, while the francs last, how about me buying you dinner?"

"Now, you mean?"

Lancaster said: "BEA didn't exactly excel themselves and I can't see the RAF offering flight service. We'll be ravenous by the time the night's out."

"I've still got a load of things to settle. I'm due at the embassy, for one thing, and I've already eaten after a fashion." Sydenham drained his glass. "Tell you what. You stay here, yes? Order a meal and spare yourself the problem of being chained up. Then, say at ten-fifteen, be on the lookout for me downstairs."

"All right."

"Outside, mind. I won't be able to leave the car. So hang about, will you? They may use a van for all I know."

"Will you have the other half before you go?"

"I'd like to, but I ought to be getting my skates on."

"Okay."

Lancaster took the chain off his wrist as soon as Sydenham left and pushed the carrying case into the bedside cabinet. It was only seven-twenty; time seemed to be stretching itself. Before ringing through about dinner he put in a call to Holland Park; McBride's injunction wasn't going to stand in the way of a few minutes' conversation, and suddenly the longing to hear Catherine was intense. There was a fifteen-minute delay on London calls and he waited impatiently, moving about the small, airless room, pulling the thick curtains aside and staring down at the traffic bunching toward the Gare de l'Est: the Paris he knew was a long way from here.

He snatched at the receiver when the call came. "Hallo, yes?"

"I have no reply from your London number."

"Are you sure?"

The ringing tone was suddenly against the shell of his ear. "That is your number," the operator said with the exasperation of one too often disbelieved. Then, after a pause: "Do you wish to cancel the call?"

Dejectedly, Lancaster said: "Yes, cancel it." The conspiracy was still in force. Once again he felt deprived and this time the feeling was stronger; in a disturbing way it amounted to one almost of abandonment. He lay askew on the bed and stared at the ceiling, remembering days when she had made no secret of her emotions, nights when her voice had broken in passion. She had warmed to him gradually, intriguing him with her reticence, a reticence so in contrast with the intensity of what was to follow that it had surprised him to discover he wasn't the first. And he could have done with some of that intensity this evening, even a distant cross-Channel hint of it. Others peopled her life, and always would; of course. But a word, a laugh, a question answered— any or all of these would have reminded him that sanity was waiting when this last hurdle was cleared; this last, lousy, futile hurdle. "You frighten me sometimes," she'd said gravely at Kilvarna, and now he had frightened himself. By the time the night was out he was going to hate himself, too; and the credit for that was hers, the cure for that was hers.

He rang down for a menu. When the room-service waiter took his order Lancaster also asked him to bring half a dozen miniature bottles of Scotch: whatever else it was sure to be a cold journey. The embassy, Sydenham had told him, would be settling with the Alexa for the room, so he dealt with his personal bill when he eventually went down to the foyer at ten o'clock. Half an hour earlier he'd hesitated about trying to reach Catherine again, finally deciding against having salt rubbed into the wound by a second disappointment.

Outside, there was already a chill in the air. With his coat on he stood by the curb, the carrying case tight under his arm. "Taxi, sir?" the commissionaire asked, and he shook his head, watching others leave and arrive, half expecting any car that drew in to be Sydenham's. He was there for twenty minutes before a black Citroën pulled up some distance from the hotel's entrance. He looked at it doubtfully: no one got out. And then a window was wound down and he heard his name called. As he approached, the front near-side door swung open. He checked the occupants before he started to climb in: Sydenham on the left in the back, a stranger in the middle, a second stranger on the right. And the driver: raincoat and soft hat like the one on the right behind. Lancaster slammed the door after him, easing into the seat. No one had said anything. The driver went into gear and they pulled away. Chance would be the middle one, but he couldn't bring himself to look around; a thin face, cropped hair, he'd seen that much.

"Where we going? A party?" Despite the amused snort the flat Midlands' voice had an awful whining quality. "Why not start at the Folies then?"

A slow shiver crawled on Lancaster's neck. In another context Conway had once asked: "What kind of bastard does these things?" Our kind, Lancaster thought. He wasn't going to be able to forget this, any of it.

Clear of the city they made their way at speed toward the flat country south of Beauvais, now tunneling under the arches of roadside plane trees, now separated from farmland only by a verge of grass, sometimes by hedges. Here and there a village flashed past like a lighted train. Near one of them the driver swore at a cat, swore and swerved, but there was a general reluctance to break the silence. Chance coughed from time to time and once he asked Sydenham for a cigarette. Later he leaned forward and touched Lancaster on the shoulder. "You English?"

"Yes."

"That's more like it. You can have these Frenchies, I can tell you. Wherever we're going I won't be sorry to see the back of this lot."

Incredibly, mercifully, it was all a mystery to him still. At a few minutes to eleven they took a side road, swinging right, headlights at full beam. By five past they were turning into a gateway and swaying along a narrow track. The moon had come up, almost full, and Lancaster could see a few low buildings crouched on the skyline. They bumped over the corrugated grain of the track for perhaps a quarter of a mile. Then a torch winked at them from away to the left and the driver changed direction, the headlights picking out another car in the lee of the nearest building, three or four standing figures and, some way beyond these, a twin-engined aircraft.

Sydenham was the first to get out; Lancaster the last. He watched Sydenham cross to the group, nod, and begin talking; watched Chance follow, out of step with his escort, the driver close on his heels. Chance was quite a small man, slightly built, and he walked with a curious spring in his step that could have indicated hope. Everyone started toward the plane. By the time Lancaster caught up with them they were already there—those from the Citroën, another anonymous civilian and, Lancaster reckoned, the RAF pilot and navigator. And an argument was under way. Chance's escort was saying to Sydenham: "You have no handcuffs of your own?"

"No. I naturally expected—"

"I can't part with these. They are the property of my department."

"I'll have them returned to you."

"I'm afraid I cannot agree to that. You and this other gentleman"—indicating Lancaster—"have no handcuffs between you? None at all?" Such inefficiency astonished him.

"No," Sydenham said tartly, "we haven't."

They were speaking in French, but Chance had got the drift. It was impossible for him not to have; his right arm had been pulled up to waist level and the release key was in the lock, held there by the escort's finger and thumb. Lancaster hadn't seen him face to face before; now their eyes met, and in that instant he experienced the first genuine stab of pity of his whole life.

"All right," Sydenham said with a gesture. "Take 'em off if you must."

"From the moment I do the onus will be yours." They might have been discussing a parcel.

"Don't worry. I've got a gun."

The handcuffs clicked open. Chance started rubbing his wrist, then bowed sardonically to the Frenchman. His skin had a moon-green pallor and he looked utterly harmless, not at all like someone with four deaths to his name.

They were airborne by eleven twenty-five, lifting off the strip in a steep climb, the runway lights which were switched on while they taxied into position vanishing almost at once afterward. The three of them sat alone to the rear of the wings, rows of empty stiff-backed seats behind and in front of them.

"VIP, eh?" Chance said with that awful snort which served as a laugh and proclaimed his nervousness. He had no overcoat. He was wearing a blue serge suit that seemed a size too large for him, a thick black pullover, crumpled white shirt and no tie. Long sinewy wrists protruded from the sleeves.

He was sitting next to Sydenham, across the aisle, and Lancaster passed them both a miniature whisky.

"Thanks," Chance said. "It was bleeding cold out there, and no mistake."

They had swung northeast and were leveled off; Paris tinted the sky away to their right. Lancaster fingered the briefcase chain, reminding himself why he was here. But for the Old Man wanting to run with the hare and hunt with the hounds he wouldn't have been. And but for Chance he wouldn't have cared. Eighteen pages of skillfully interlocked lies were his responsibility; Chance was Sydenham's. Yet the credit for both was his and he wished to God he could harden his heart. With Walker he had, with Hearne he had. They were alive, after all; and they'd achieved something. He wanted to ask Sydenham exactly what would happen at Feldhagen, but it was impossible now, and in any case a part of him shrank from knowing.

"Cigarette?" Lancaster leaned across the aisle. Sydenham shook his head but Chance took one.

"I'll need a match, too." He lowered his lips toward the stem of flame as if he thirsted. "Thought I'd never smoke a filter again. What they let me have took the back of your throat out." He picked at his lower lip as if expecting to find a strand of tobacco; the cigarette he gripped in his teeth. "D'you know the kind?"

"I think so."

The plane bucked a little, the wings quivering in the moonlight. Lancaster emptied his bottle.

Chance said presently: "What's all this about, mister? Can you tell me?" Lancaster pretended not to hear, looking away, blowing smoke. "It's been go, go, go all day and no one's explained yet. Well, those Frenchies jabbered at me when I asked, but what use was that? I don't understand a bleeding word of the lingo except 'Voulez-vous jig-a-jig?' and 'Combien?' or something." The snort again, more apprehensive now. "What's up, eh? What's this caper in aid of?"

Lancaster glanced sidelong at Sydenham, but Sydenham stared ahead. The urge was to say: "Ask him. You're his, not mine." Instead he answered: "You're being transferred."

"I can see that. But where? What for?" After a pause Chance tried again. "Are we going home?" Then: "I'm with the British now, aren't I? I'm going to be with the British, aren't I?"

"Yes," Lancaster said. "You're going to be with the British." He shot another glance at Sydenham, like an angry plea for help, then turned away, prickling, watching the slow slide of the land and the clustered lights of towns where life went on.

They must have made up time. Soon after one they were noticeably lower. Lancaster's ears seemed clogged. What could have been Hanover showed far to the left and they were canting over, veering south, seeming to search for a line. Chance had dozed, but he stirred now as the engine note deepened, suddenly awake, condemned-cell alertness printed at once on the bony, ignorant features.

"Is this it?"

"Must be."

By a miracle he didn't ask where. Wheels down, flaps down; they came in smoothly, scarcely jarring. There were trees well back to either side, at least one other runway, a string of buildings ahead as they rocked along the dispersal lane. Lancaster dug into his coat pocket and brought out the remaining miniatures.

"Here," he said, and passed them to Chance.

"Thanks, mister. Something for the road, eh?"

"That kind of thing."

They lurched to a standstill. The pilot opened the cabin door. "Journey's end, gentlemen. O-one-fourteen and all's well."

A car was swinging eagerly across the hard as they unbelted themselves, coming in obedience to the realization of a suggestion better never made. Lancaster stood up woodenly, chained to the case as implacably as Chance was chained to the next few hours.

# Chapter 15 ] ✦

THE car looked yellowish under
the moon. The squat lieutenant-colonel who greeted them
addressed himself to Sydenham. "Morning. I'm Rouse."
Greatcoat, gloves, General List cap-badge; a dewdrop on the
end of his nose which he brushed away. It was colder here
than near Beauvais; ten degrees or so lower.

Chance shivered as it penetrated. "Why the army? What's
the sodding army got to do with me?"

"Take it easy," Sydenham said.

"Where the hell am I going?" He was frightened at last,
the whine more marked. "Can't anyone answer a simple
bleeding question?"

"Let's get in, shall we?" Rouse said. "It's perishing here."

Sydenham shoved Chance gently. "In the back with me."

Rouse joined them. As before, Lancaster sat beside the
driver, a tough, fresh-faced corporal who chewed incessantly.

"Where are we?" Chance demanded, peering out. "This
isn't England, is it? Come on, somebody—is it?"

"You're in Germany," Rouse said, as if surprised he didn't
know.

"Germany? Christ!" Then: "Why? Why Germany? Answer me that."

[ 228 ]

No one did. The car was moving.

"Sod you. All of you."

A gate was opened, the sentry saluting as they nosed clear. Rouse said: "We're behind the clock, corporal. Do the best you can, will you?" And the corporal stopped chewing long enough to grunt, "Yes, sir."

He drove for forty minutes, mostly very fast. They seemed to avoid towns of any size. The roads were good and straight but they didn't keep to any particular one for long. Several times they changed direction, dog-legging eastward, the night all theirs except for a stray vehicle or two and, once, a group of army trucks moving in convoy. Chance opened the three remaining miniatures in turn, and the whisky gave him a certain defiance.

"When we get where we're going I want to see someone, someone at the top. I'm entitled to an explanation, and I'm damned well going to have one, if it's the last thing I do." He was slurring his words a bit. "Who are you people, anyhow? And, for the hundredth time, where in the blazes are you taking me?"

"You're going to Feldhagen," Rouse said.

"Where's that? Feldhagen doesn't mean a thing to me. What for?"

"You'll have everything explained there."

It was the nearest anyone had come to even the beginnings of the truth, yet it quieted him. Lancaster had never imagined that being with him would seem so endless, the litany of his questions so intolerable. The tension had increased the farther they traveled. There must have been other ways of trying to salvage Roman Candle in the time.

*Must have been. . . .* No wonder the Old Man had shunned this.

Frost glittered on the roads and fields now. They went left, then right, then left again, and eventually a sign announced that they were entering Feldhagen. It was only a village, larger than some they'd passed, but that didn't mean much. Lancaster greeted it with relief. They cruised through a cobbled square; there was an inn on one side, a dark, balconied building with a clock tower on the other. Twelve minutes after two.

"Not bad," Rouse muttered. "Not bad at all." To Sydenham he said: "About a mile more."

The village receded. The driver had cut to sidelights only, Lancaster noted, and instinctively he looked left, wondering where the frontier was; but all he saw were beet fields and clumps of trees. The road made two sharp bends, suddenly disclosing a post-and-rail fence on the right; beyond it stood three or four army huts, closely spaced, set in a U-shape in front of a flagstaff.

"By the guardhouse, corporal."

They pulled up. No one came to meet them. Rouse left the car and went along the short path to the central hut door. Light showed as he opened it and went in. A minute later he returned with someone else; a sergeant of the military police.

"You can hand over now, Sydenham."

"Listen," Chance began. "I want a word with somebody."

"All in good time," Rouse said evenly.

"What's the game? Who's this fellow?"

"Come on." Rouse's voice suddenly had a bite. "Hurry it up."

The command had its effect on Chance; he was probably used to commands. He clambered out, looking scared again, alarm in his stance and his eyes and his bony face.

"Take him away, sergeant."

"Sir."

Lancaster watched them go into the guardhouse; all the spring had gone out of Chance's step. As soon as the door closed Lancaster said to Rouse, "My instructions were to part with the documents directly Chance was in your charge." He wanted the damn thing off his wrist, to be shot of it, shot of it all.

"I'm not quite ready for them yet, if you don't mind."

Rouse had a pencil-thin moustache which Lancaster hadn't noticed before. They had hardly spoken until now. "When will you be?"

"Half an hour?" A bleak smile, shadowed by his cap.

Sydenham was stamping his feet. "Perhaps we can wait somewhere, then."

"I'd rather both you gentlemen came with me. This is your affair, after all, and I'd like you to see what's been laid on."

"I hardly think that's necessary," Lancaster said.

"It's only a few hundred yards. We'll have him brought forward soon. And his clothes are up there."

"Clothes?"

"What he'll be wearing."

"D'you mean to say—?"

"He'll change? Yes. He'll need to look the part." Rouse added bluntly: "You can spoil a ship for a ha-porth of tar, you know." He was a soldier; obeyed orders. For him there were no complications.

"Oh Christ," Lancaster said.

"And the stuff you're carrying will be sewn to the underwear we've provided. So hang on until we arrive and I've shown you both the setup."

It was as if Rouse had chosen to rub Lancaster's nose in revulsion. They walked side by side to begin with, briskly, then in single file when Rouse turned off the road onto a track. Trees hemmed them in, pines. After three or four minutes the track funneled out into the open. The wire barrier of the frontier was directly ahead, stretching from left to right. Beyond it was another barrier, higher, more severe, with two lookout towers. What appeared to be a farm cottage was within a few yards of the nearer fence and Rouse led them toward it. "O.P.," he said quietly, expanding on that for the benefit of civilians. "Observation post."

A smudge of smoke rose from the single chimney; the windows were covered. There was a ladder, a permanent fixture, at the rear of the cottage, which led to a platform built across the slope of the roof.

"No cigarettes, please."

They followed Rouse up and stood looking at the strip between East and West. The quiet there was like someone on tiptoes, holding his breath. And it seemed to intensify as Rouse began to spell out the pattern of Chance's annihilation.

He kept his voice right down.

"The distance between their wire and ours is a hundred and ten yards. They've two watchtowers, as you see, and they're about four hundred yards apart. They used to mine their side of the strip at one time, but not any more—not here, that is. This is because of the cemetery way over there to the right." He pointed into the silvery distance. "The cemetery straddles the strip, and in recent years they've allowed Feldhagen people to cross on certain days to tend family graves and what have you.

"Now, if you look half left, nine o'clock say, you'll notice something—some old farm equipment, harrow I think it is, rusted to hell. Dead in front of us are two oak trees and another slightly to their right. There's also a depression in the ground—d'you see it?—at one o'clock. These—the harrow, the trees and the depression—provide the only worthwhile cover."

He was speaking about an operation that was going to be carried out in a certain way.

"Our own dispositions will be as follows. Two men will be sited on the bank down there, below us and to the left. Another will be up here, where we are now, and two more at ground level a short distance away to the right; you can't quite see where I mean, but they'll be up against the wire and able to fire through it. They're top-class, all of them."

"And Chance?" Sydenham asked.

"Will go through the gap directly in front of the cottage."

Lancaster licked his lips. "Like a coursing hare," McBride had said. And then another voice echoed, Conway's: "He's going to be executed anyway, Andrew . . ." Even so, even so. This was no place to be. He glanced across at Sydenham, hoping to discover a glimpse of what he himself was feeling, but Sydenham seemed more concerned with the cold than anything.

"We patrol this stretch for a couple of miles in either

direction," Rouse was saying. "It's dull, uneventful routine, and has been for years. For that reason it is absolutely vital that we play our cards right."

"How d'you mean?"

"Any hint of this having been laid on will give the game away. Over there they patrol with a vengeance and they've searchlights in those towers. The least bit of trouble on their side and they go into action like a dose of salts: they're ten times more suspicious than we are. Someone tried to cross about three months ago and they had him before he'd covered twenty yards. But they won't expect that from us. We've got to appear to improvise our fire. There mustn't seem to be anything ad hoc about it. And, furthermore, we somehow have to allow him to get as close to their side as possible."

A cloud dragged over the moon and the night contracted sharply. Within a minute it had passed, but Rouse didn't wait. He knew what was out there like the back of his hand.

"There are three ways Chance will go. Either he'll make for the harrow, or the trees, or the depression. My bet is he'll go for the trees, but it won't much matter which he chooses. We can cover him all the way. My fellows will be sited for any eventuality. What's more important is the manner in which we let the incident develop. It's got to *happen*—as far as we're concerned, that is. So this is the way we'll play it." He wiped another dewdrop away with the back of his gloved hand. "We'll let him cover about thirty yards, then the man up here will give a warning shout. It's normal for us to have someone on this platform at various times during the night, and they know it. A shout then, followed by a single shot —merely to get the action started. The shot will come from here and it will go wide. Then there will be another shout and some scrambling activity down below, followed by a second sighting shot from one of the men close to the wire."

His voice wasn't carrying more than a few yards.

"Now it could be that they'll turn their searchlights on. Whether they will or not remains to be seen, but I'd say it's probable—not to pick out Chance, of course, but to try and blind us. If they're quick they might attempt that—it's an old standby—and this is where they'll concentrate their attention, here, and perhaps where the second shot will have come from. But they can't be everywhere with their lights at once, and Chance will be halfway over by then—either nearing the trees, or by the harrow, or making for the depression. And that's when the men on the bank will come into their own. They'll be able to pick him off whichever route he selects, searchlights or no. The depression's very shallow; you can rake it from the bank, and we've got three pretty conclusive angles on to the trees. . . . By that time the shooting will seem to be as haphazard as can possibly be, as if we'd almost been caught with our trousers down. At least, that's the object of the exercise."

He turned, as if from a sandtable. "Any questions?" And both Lancaster and Sydenham shook their heads.

"These fellows of mine are the best there are. There's no danger of coming unstuck on that score. The trick's going to be in making it seem to happen plausibly."

Sydenham muttered: "In the best muddle-through traditions."

"That's it," Rouse said, oblivious of the barb. "That's exactly it."

He led the way down the ladder. Lancaster took a last look

over the peak of the roof before descending after Sydenham, knowing as he did so that the scene would haunt him as long as he lived, pity already evolving into shame, shame such as even Catherine would never be able to eradicate. Hard? Not this hard. What he had achieved in the past had been done by nerve and by memory, using a go-between; there had been no codes, no microfilms, no hidden compartments, no technical subtleties, no professional skills. Nerve and memory and self-control, these were his only weapons; these, and crude incriminations at periods of crisis. And they had led him here, led Chance here. Nothing was worth this.

"What happens now?" Sydenham asked Rouse, tight-lipped. He seemed a little confused.

"You'd better come back to the guardhouse with me."

"And then?"

"We'll have him brought up."

Lancaster said: "Does he know yet?"

"Know?"

"Has he been told?"

"Not yet."

"Who will do that?" They were in a group, at the foot of the ladder, their breath frosting on the air. "You?"

"No, thank God," Rouse answered in the same clipped voice that then and then only might have masked any feeling. "No, it won't be me."

"Who, then?" This was Sydenham, frowning.

They had begun to move, and Rouse didn't reply. Instead, turning to Lancaster, he said: "There's no point in your coming along. I think it would be best if you waited here until we return."

" 'We'?" Sydenham said.

"That's for you to decide." Then, to Lancaster again: "There's a stove inside the cottage. I'd warm up, if I were you. You'll be hanging about for a quarter of an hour or so yet."

"All right," Lancaster nodded.

He stood watching Rouse and Sydenham traipse away; the cottage covered them from the watchtowers. When they were into the trees he walked around to the side of the building where slivers of light framed a door. Someone moved in a shadow-filled angle of the wall. "Who's there?" Peering, Lancaster saw an armed soldier.

"Colonel Rouse told me to wait inside."

"Your name?"

"Lancaster."

"Okay. Shut the door quick after you."

Warmth met Lancaster directly he opened it. He went in sideways, not looking around until he'd clipped the door back on its latch. Then he turned, blinking into an oil lamp's glow at the centrally placed stove where a man stood warming his hands. And with disbelief he saw it was McBride and knew instantly, as alarm broke over him in a cold wave, that something had gone terribly wrong.

"Hallo, sir." He was rooted by the door. "I . . . I didn't expect to find you here." The smile that had succeeded so often was a disaster now.

McBride straightened by the stove. "There's been a change of plan, David."

"Oh?"

"Chance isn't going over."

"Not going? But surely . . ." Lancaster moved his free

hand, still in the grip of shock and suspicion, searching madly in his mind for what McBride's presence meant. "Does Rouse know? I was with him until a minute ago, and—"

"He knows."

"It's off, then? Is that it?"

"On the contrary. The only change concerns Chance. You see, David, we're putting you over in his place."

# Chapter 16 ] 

"**I**T'S finished, David."

Lancaster's voice, when it came, didn't sound like his own; his lips seemed glued to his teeth. "I don't understand," he faltered. But he did, and a part of him quailed, terrified. "What's all this about? Rouse and Sydenham and I . . ." He couldn't stop himself. "Why are you here?"

"I'm here to sum up," McBride said. "And I asked especially for the privilege. It's all over, David. You're done for. Roman Candle and you have gone full circle."

"I don't know what you're talking about." A pace forward; another spreading gesture of the right hand, his left chained to the briefcase. "Roman Candle? This is preposterous."

"Far from it."

"But it is. It *is*, I tell you." His raised voice fluttered around the room, a room that he was blind to; all he saw was McBride.

And McBride said: "If it were, you and I wouldn't be face to face at this moment." He hadn't moved. For what seemed an unbearable amount of time there was silence, a silence broken only by the soldier shuffling his feet outside. Sweat was oozing in icy beads from Lancaster's forehead.

"You must be crazy, sir," he tried desperately. "Are you suggesting—"

"I'm suggesting nothing. I'm dealing with facts. Known facts, the major one being that you have consistently fed secret information to a foreign power."

"I?"

"Yes, David, you."

"That's a monstrous accusation. I deny it."

"Naturally. Your kind always do—as I remarked when we discussed Stephen Hearne." With that shattering, destructive force of his the Old Man went on: "What you pulled on Hearne wasn't very clever. It had the hallmark of the amateur, which is what you are, you know. An amateur. And amateurs should never pit themselves against professionals. Deep water is for those who can swim."

"Everything you're saying is meaningless to me. Utterly meaningless."

"Come now," McBride said in a chiding tone. "Let's drop this, shall we? We haven't long, and you're entitled to an explanation."

Fear moved in Lancaster anew as he thought of the calculated nightmare waiting beyond the wire. It couldn't be for him. *Couldn't be.* The Old Man would never permit it. Not that. . . . He took another pace forward and McBride seemed to move in and out of focus with every sickening beat of his heart. He couldn't grasp that McBride was an enemy. Conway, yes; Sloan, yes; almost anyone else, yes. But not McBride.

"Listen," he began.

"You listen." Something crackled inside the stove. "You remember Walker? Well, in certain quarters there was uneasiness about what happened to Walker. Not at first, but later, as the months went by. You were in my department by then and—I give you credit for this—for a longish time your behavior couldn't be faulted. We were very unsure of ourselves, I can tell you. Despite your close connection with Walker, for a while you seemed most unlikely to bear fruit."

"This is make-believe, all of it."

"If only it were." McBride closed his eyes. "Eight months ago, almost to the day, C.I.A. reported a leak on Roman Candle. Eight months ago, David—well before we invented Adler."

"Invented?"

"Invented, yes. We've invented so much, d'you see? Does it shock you so?"

"You're lying."

"We focused on you in the spring. But your amateur talent disarmed us even then. We still weren't entirely certain, not for quite a while, not until quite recently in fact. So we invented Adler as a means of putting the pressure on. And, after a fashion, I suppose one could say we succeeded."

Outside, the soldier coughed. The door was as good as barred.

"I doubt if there's ever been anyone quite like you in your chosen line. Only Blake did more damage. Given time and a full rein I'm certain that you would have put him in the shade. Of its type, Roman Candle is far and away the best weapon this country has ever perfected; and Discus promises to be even more so. You had great opportunities, David, and you would have had others. The disaster, from your viewpoint, is that what you've passed in recent weeks has been garbled before it reached your hands."

Lancaster swayed.

"You must have come close to suspecting it on occasions; when Norris let slip that mention of the P-Five's intended use, for instance. But that's by the way, now. And such harm as you did before we really had your number will be put right in the fashion you yourself suggested. Which is ironic, to say the least. And we've been a little less crude than you might imagine. All likely embassies are being watched sufficiently openly for the fact to be noticed. Fletcher's arrest has been made public. There'll therefore be an acceptable reason for what will seem to them an act of panic on your part, and this will be strengthened by our subsequently admitting that you were on a visit to Germany for discussions. Chance was a pretty poor second best, really. On the other hand they'll know you over there. Your face won't be that of a stranger."

"You can't mean this."

"No? . . . Cast your mind back, David. Consider what you thought was expedient when you believed you were working all of us on strings. You were ready to protect your own position by incriminating others. But two lives torn apart weren't enough. You went further. You were prepared to have another butchered in the same cause."

"Chance is a murderer. And besides—"

Terrified, Lancaster began to speak of regret, shame, trying to convey that his senses had been revolted; looking as he did so for a glimpse of compassion in return; but there was only steel in the Old Man's eyes, coldness, and even as Lancaster protested he realized with horror that this was all there had ever been. And yet he went stumbling on, des-

perate to rediscover what he had always believed was friendship, softness, frailty.

"It's late in the day, David." McBride shook his head.

"You must understand! I want to tell you—"

"It will alter nothing."

"There must be charges, specific charges. A trial . . . I
have the right to a trial."

"Your rights have already ended."

"I'm innocent," Lancaster shouted through his fear. "Innocent."

An insect flew against the lamp and glanced off; there was
no end to life. Still the Old Man did not move.

"Listen," he said, and his voice was as gentle as ever. "You
know too much. Far, far too much. And a jail sentence is no
use. They'd either get you out or exchange you in a few years,
and we never intended to risk either—not in your case. So we
invented Adler, and Sloan waited to see which way you'd
jump. Hearne nobody reckoned on. And Chance was someone I doubt if even Merton would have thought up. But since
you did, and since you were to be disposed of, we developed
the idea. We invented Chance, too; the person you've es-
corted, that is. The real Chance is still presumably in Bordeaux. The French were in no way involved, except for the
use of the emergency field near Beauvais, and that was under a NATO provision. . . . Others can work strings, David."

"You'll gain nothing by this. Nothing, d'you hear?"

"You think not?"

"Every scrap on Roman Candle has already reached
them. Last weekend. Everything. Straight off the files. . . .
What's more they know about your rescue operation. They

*know,* don't you understand? They know someone's crossing with this"—Lancaster brandished the briefcase—"and that it's to be ignored. What's been arranged out there will be for nothing. Nothing." Lancaster paused, his trump played, the only one. And for a second or two hope flickered.

"You admit to this, but maintain you are innocent? You tell me Chance was to have been thrown away to no purpose, and yet you can say that you are sorry for him?"

"I never imagined it would be like this."

The Old Man gazed at him impassively. All he might have pitied was the flesh, which at least was like his own. He might have pitied the agony in the eyes, the hunted look already planted there. But that was all. The rest he couldn't pity because he couldn't make identification.

"Your friends over there know nothing, David."

"Oh yes they do."

"I can promise you they don't. We stamped on Fletcher a week ago. Last Thursday, to be exact."

"You're bluffing."

"Why should I be? I'll elaborate on Fletcher if you insist. His real name is Fleischer—or perhaps you weren't aware of that? Fleischer, Fletcher, sometimes Martin Brain, care of the Tythe Barn Inn, Lisdoonvarna. In the Republic of Ireland. Is that a bluff, do you think?"

Lancaster seemed to wilt. He leaned against the bare table between them.

"In some respects you were an ingenious pair. Your very obviousness didn't make it easy for us. But we got the proof we needed in the end, and I don't mean as late as last Thursday. From your own mouth." McBride waited. "A lady's compact—surely you remember? You carried it for her

sometimes. And sometimes you and Fletcher were alone together, even in public."

"No!" Lancaster's mouth twitched as his eyes widened in
a blaze of dismay. "Oh Christ, no!"

"It was a recording unit, David."

"No!"

"Miss Tierney didn't join Weapons Coordination merely
to be George Conway's secretary."

Lancaster stared, McBride forgotten, Fletcher forgotten,
those he had served forgotten. There were other ways of
dying; something in him was shriveling away to nothing.

"I don't believe you. I won't. . . . We love each other."
His shoulders were shaking, all vestige of control finally going. "We love each other. . . ."

"What do you know about love?"

No answer. Footsteps were nearing the cottage.

"What is love?" the Old Man said rhetorically.

He walked around the table to the door, turning there for
a moment before letting himself out. But emotion was a lux-
ury he had never allowed himself.


They made Lancaster strip down to his underwear, then
went through his pockets and tacked the plastic envelope
containing the photocopies to the inside of his shirt. They
were considerate about it and moved him close to the stove
because he was shivering. Someone said afterward that he
didn't seem to care what they were doing. He didn't speak,
or protest, or struggle, but nobody recalled his expression
because they couldn't bring themselves to look him in the
face. A few items were returned to his pockets after examina-
tion and the only thing to be kept back was his coat; instead

they gave him a grayish boiler suit, neither new nor old, which buttoned up to his neck.

It was exactly six minutes after three o'clock when he went through the gap in the wire in front of the cottage. There wasn't a cloud within reach of the moon; they'd been careful about that. He seemed to go quite willingly, in a kind of stupor. At first he walked, hands to his sides, gazing ahead. There was no urgency in his stride. After about a dozen paces he hesitated, stopped, then began to turn as if gripped by the most awful burst of fear, lifting his arms in what might have been a gesture of appeal. And, immediately, Rouse's plan went into operation.

A hoarse shout came from the platform, followed almost at once by the crack of a rifle shot. Soil erupted within inches of where Lancaster was standing and it had the effect of spinning him around; something seemed to snap in him and he started to run, head down, crouching, making for the trees.

He would have heard the hubbub that suddenly began near the cottage: voices, the scamper of feet, a door banging. And he would have known that the next shot would also go wide. The stage directions would have been in his thoughts as he ran, wits resurrecting, yet he started to jink and swerve before the second sighter was loosed off from ground level. It came like a handclap, struck something and ricocheted; at the wire they heard its sobbing whine. And they heard, too, as he would have heard, the startled voices on the other side, the barked command from one of the watchtowers.

Everything was beginning to happen at once, yet in a dreadful kind of slow motion. Forty yards from the cottage

Lancaster tripped and went sprawling; he was then only about twenty yards from the nearest tree. As he scrambled frantically to his feet a beam of light broke from the left-hand tower, sweeping from side to side, brushing over him then swinging back, holding him as if in bewildered discovery, a dazzling fuzz outlining his silhouette. Simultaneously he began running again, stumbling, bawling "No! No!" with an arm thrown up to ward off the blinding glare. For a split-second longer the light imprisoned him, then darted abruptly away; and in the same instant another flashed from the right-hand tower, focusing full on the cottage and holding there.

To those on the platform Lancaster seemed to vanish for a moment. But from the bank he was clearly visible, within feet of the trees, bent low under the streaming fingers of light, and the first man who fired in earnest was surprised he only got him through the shoulder. Lancaster went down as if he'd been kicked, clutching himself; he rolled a couple of times, then was up again, canted forward. He was more than halfway across by this time, running like a man in possession of the ball with only the fullback to beat. Rouse yelled at those in the vital crossfire position on the bank to take him again, but the beam of the other searchlight ceased to wander and swung uncertainly in their direction, wavering to and fro along the line of the fence, helping to lose him.

Lancaster seemed to sense that the plan had miscarried. Suddenly, he changed direction, going right, toward the cemetery. He was about thirty yards from the far wire, moving parallel to it, still sidestepping, still crouched as if unable to recover his balance. They were calling to him now from the other side, harsh German voices, but he didn't turn toward them; everything Rouse had said would have been racing through his mind—angles, distance, timing. Two more shots cracked in hurried succession from the bank, but by the wire below the cottage it was seen that he wasn't hit.

And then the men Rouse had never mentioned opened up. They were positioned on the western edge of the cemetery and they were absolutely unhampered by the searchlights, able to hold Lancaster in their sights as he staggered across their front.

The first bullet must have struck him in the side. He crumpled up as if he'd gone headlong into a wall, and for a moment or two he didn't move. The searchlights were sweeping everywhere now and there was an awful wailing noise rising from farther along the far fence, like a warning maroon on a foggy river. It seemed to rouse him, as if he'd recollected something. In the moonlight they could see him raise his head and start to crawl. And he probably managed several feet before another bullet smashed into him and Rouse knew for sure that it was all over.

On the watchtowers they realized it, too. The piercing beams were abruptly extinguished, leaving only the pale, motionless moonlight. The sound of the alarm died as if it were being slowly throttled. An intense quiet flooded in once more, seeming to come from the very ends of the earth. And on it there wasn't so much as a whisper of Lancaster's ever having lived.

# Chapter 17 ] 🦋

McBRIDE walked slowly to where his car was waiting. He walked with his hands thrust deep into his overcoat pockets. Sydenham, at his shoulder, silently urged him to move at a brisker pace. His own face was pinched with the cold and his teeth kept chattering; he felt a little sick. But McBride took his time. The frost crackled underfoot and their breath hung like gauze on the still air. Neither of them spoke. Neither of them had exchanged a word since leaving the observation platform.

The car was a quarter of a mile from the cottage, in a side lane. The driver saw them coming and jumped out to open up.

"Had the engine running, sir, on and off. Otherwise you'd have been starting in an icebox."

They clambered in and the doors slammed.

"Airport, sir?"

"No." McBride seemed to come back from an enormous distance. "This gentleman wants to be taken to the inn first."

"The one in the village?"

"That's right," Sydenham said. "Opposite the Town Hall." He couldn't remember having been so cold.

"Is your colleague there?" McBride asked him.

"Yes. We'll be going back tomorrow."

"Where did you get him from? Is he one of your people?"

Sydenham nodded. "We went over to Paris together the day before yesterday."

They rode in silence for a while. Telegraph poles flicked past, like gibbets against the blanched sky. The lane severed a main road and the driver swung left. The lights of Feldhagen were showing now.

It was a big car. Sydenham stopped rubbing his gloved hands and leaned forward; slid the glass partition across, sealing them in. The sickness was still with him and it wasn't from the cold. He'd never seen anyone killed before, and he'd been party to it.

"I didn't know it was going to be him. No one told me that."

He might have been talking to himself.

"In any case it was murder," he said quietly.

McBride moved his head. "No."

"No?"

"An execution."

"For what?"

"Treason."

"Treason no longer carries the death penalty."

"In time of war."

"But there's no war. We aren't at war."

"Some of us are," McBride said. "For some of us it has never stopped, and that includes your department."

Sydenham stared at him, but McBride's face was masked by shadows. Only the voice provided any sort of clue—soft, tired, yet iron-hard and fulfilled.

"Who decides these things?"

There was no reply. They were into the village.

"Who decided about this? You?" Sydenham ventured.

McBride moved in his seat. "No, it wasn't me."

"Who, then? Who said: 'Yes, go ahead'?"

The car had begun bumping over the cobbles in the square.

"Don't ask," McBride said. "It doesn't pay to ask. You'll never get an answer."

"Who engineered it, then? Who put the idea forward in the first place?"

The lights of the inn fell on them as the wheels nudged the curb, and Sydenham looked very young by contrast, a little frightened, as if he were only just beginning to realize the strength of the secret that bound him, and of others that might bind him yet.

"Good night," McBride said as the driver opened the door.

"Was it you?"

"Good night, Sydenham."

They left him standing on the steps of the inn, alone, gazing mutely after them. "The airport now, sir?"

"Please."

"There was a spot of trouble just then, wasn't there? I was in the car, but I thought I heard shooting."

"Oh?" McBride said.

He settled back. Only now was he becoming aware of the cold; it was in his bones. And he thought of the fire Catherine Tierney had once told him about, and Lancaster bending to stoke it with wood and watching the insects run from the flames.